# *Stories* for the *Seasons*

## *24* tales of --

courage

sacrifice

compassion

redemption

resurrection

## CHUCK WARZYN

authorHOUSE®

*AuthorHouse™*
*1663 Liberty Drive*
*Bloomington, IN 47403*
*www.authorhouse.com*
*Phone: 1-800-839-8640*

*First published by AuthorHouse 12/30/2010*

*ISBN: 978-1-4520-9225-6 (sc)*
*ISBN: 978-1-4520-9226-3 (dj)*
*ISBN: 978-1-4520-9227-0 (e)*

*Library of Congress Control Number: 2010916992*

*Printed in the United States of America*

*This book is printed on acid-free paper.*

*Certain stock imagery © Thinkstock.*

# Table of Contents

# CHRISTMAS

❄ ❄ ❄

# GIFTS FOR THE CHILD

*(The inspiration for this short story was an item I read in a newspaper many years ago that quoted a man on a Christmastime city street who approached a sidewalk Santa Claus and asked how much it would cost for the Santa to come to his home and tell his daughter she was pretty. Over the years, I wondered what that question might have entailed, and so decided to expand on it and write this story. I invite the reader to identify the literary device I use in the middle of the story to suggest the magical powers of this special and holy season.)*

"How much y'all charge to say 'Ho ho ho' to my little girl an' tell her she's purty?"

The sidewalk Santa Claus stopped ringing his bell and stared at the man shivering in a denim jacket and ball cap. Around them, last-minute shoppers hurried between stores. Cars crept through the courthouse square, searching for elusive parking spaces.

The man saw the hesitation in the sidewalk Santa's face.

"She's a good kid. She just ... she always been kinda plain ... not even plain, I guess. We ain't lived here long and kids at school been teasin' 'er. She's feelin' right down tonight of all nights, an' got a cold too, and I thought mebbe ..."

"Well, sure," the sidewalk Santa replied. "Be glad to. But I gotta stay here for a coupla more hours. If you can come back ..."

"We don't live that far away," the man said in a weary voice. "Look, I'm parked right over yonder. We can put your gear in the back o' my truck. Won't take 20-25 minutes."

He reached for his wallet, pulled out a bill, and handed it to the Santa Claus.

"Look, I'll be glad to pay ya."

The Santa glanced at the money. It was a $20 bill. He smiled, took the money, and stuck it into a pocket in his costume. Picking up his collection pot and tripod, he smiled. "I'm your man. Let's go."

The Santa and the man walked to a rusting pickup, lifted the pot and tripod into the back, and climbed into the cab.

They drove along a highway leading off the square and turned onto a dead-end street lined with crackerbox houses, trash-filled yards, and carports cluttered with cardboard boxes and sagging furniture. A car up on cinderblocks in one yard reflected flashing colored lights strung from nearby houses.

The truck pulled into one of the smaller houses toward the end of the street. As the two men walked up the sidewalk to the front door, the Santa Claus looked at several painted plywood figures – the shepherds, wise men, animals, and Mary and Joseph kneeling by a manger holding the baby Jesus.

The man held the door open for Santa Claus. "I'll be right back," he said, and disappeared down a hallway.

Santa looked around the living room. A tree with ornaments and lights stood in a corner. Several boxes wrapped in what appeared to be Sunday comic strips sat under the tree. On the wall next to Santa hung a faded photograph of a man and woman holding a baby.

The man poked his head around the corner. "OK," he said. "I told her she got a special visitor. Come on back."

In the bedroom, a table lamp shone a circle of light on a girl propped up against a pile of pillows. Several books and stuffed animals, and a box of tissues clustered on the blanket around her.

The girl gasped when she saw Santa Claus, and her eyes shown wide. Santa had to keep from staring at her. He understood now why her classmates teased her.

The man had walked over to the girl and placed his hand gently on her shoulder.

"Honey, Santa said he weren't so busy tonight, he couldn't come by an' say howdy to you."

He looked back at Santa Claus with an expression that mixed concern and hope.

Santa glanced out the window onto the front lawn, onto the plywood scene of that special night in Bethlehem centuries before. He looked back at the girl. Slowly, he walked over to the bed, sat down next to her, and gently took her hands into his.

The child stared up at him and whispered, "Hello, Santa Claus."

Santa asked, "What's your name, little angel?"

"Carol," she murmured, looking down and then back up again.

"Carol," Santa Claus repeated. "Like a Christmas carol?"

The girl giggled and Santa responded with a "Ho ho ho!"

The girl began sneezing and reached for a tissue. She blew her nose as Santa reached out and patted her shoulder.

"Well, Carol; you are a very sweet, little Christmas angel," he said softly. "I wish I could stay here and visit longer with you. But, I gotta lot o' things to do before my reindeer an' me make our trip 'round the world."

"That's OK, Santa," she whispered. "I done told Daddy what I want for Christmas."

Santa Claus glanced over at the man, who nodded slightly and winked.

"Well, Christmas Carol," Santa said; "you are a very, very special young lady, and between me and your daddy, we'll see to it that you get what you want."

"Thank you, Santa Claus," she replied.

Santa gave her hand a final squeeze. Leaning forward, he kissed her forehead. Standing up, he followed the man out of the dimly lit room. He paused at the doorway, looked back at the girl, and smiled.

"Merry Christmas, Carol."

"Merry Christmas, Santa Claus. I love you."

Santa started, raised his hand in farewell, and followed the girl's father down the hallway toward the front door.

The man and the sidewalk Santa drove back to the town square in silence. Snowflakes began to fall. The dancing flakes shown like silver confetti in the beam of the truck's headlights.

The man helped the Santa unload his pot and tripod, and place them back on the sidewalk. The man gripped the Santa's hand tightly and said in a tight voice, "Thank you. You don't know how much that meant to her. And to me."

The man turned, walked back to his truck, and drove off in the night air muffled by the falling snow.

The Santa Claus looked down at his hand that the man had shaken. It contained a $5 and a $10 bill. He stuffed them into his pocket and felt the other money already nestled there. He took out all three bills, stared at them for several seconds, and placed them in his collection pot.

The snow began to come down faster. The clock in the courthouse tower chimed out the new hour as the sidewalk Santa's voice rang like a crystal bell across the town square, "Merry Christmas! Ho ho ho! Merry Christmas, everyone!"

# ANTONIO AND THE CHRISTMAS ANGELS

"Just a moment, Antonio."

The boy walked back to where his mother had stopped in front of a store window. He put down the two shopping bags and looked at the ornament-covered tree. Clustered on shelves around it were framed pictures, china figurines, animals of crystal and wood, and assorted brass items.

His mother pointed to a brass piano lamp. "Wouldn't that look just lovely on my old pump organ," she said. She leaned toward the window and adjusted her glasses. "But, my land, $69. Close to $75 with tax. Who can afford such a price?" She stood back up and smiled at her son. "Why would I want anything else for Christmas when I have a strong young son to help me as much as you do?"

Antonio looked around quickly. "Oh, Mama; someone might hear. Can't we just go on home now?" She laughed as they continued along the sidewalk toward the projects. "Don't worry, son. I don't think any of your homeboys were around to hear me."

That evening, walking home from the movie theater with his sister, Antonio paused to look at the brass piano lamp. What a great Christmas present for his mother. But he had only $20 left hidden in his bottom drawer from his job last summer helping Uncle Desmond clear out more land for his cattle.

"What you lookin' at, 'tonio?" his sister asked. "It's cold. I wanna go home. I'm tired."

"Hush your mouth, Toya," he snapped. "You oughta be glad I let Mama talk me into takin' you to the movie. Come on." The girl ran to catch up with him, and grabbed his hand. "Don't go so fast, 'tonio." He shook his head. "Girl, you a real pain, know that? Come on. I'll give you a piggyback ride home."

Antonio waited until the following evening, when his mother had gone to choir practice, before phoning his uncle. "Sorry, boy," Desmond said. "I'd like to help you out, but there just ain't any work around here now for you. Don't worry, though. Smart fella like you; you'll figure out a way to get that piano lamp for Marcella."

Middle school was out for the holidays the next day. After his mother had left for work, Antonio put his $20 into a pocket and headed for the rows of stores and businesses on the highways leading into town. The usual Saturday morning group was gathering at the basketball court as he walked by. "Later, man!" he replied to their shouts to join the game.

His first stop was the shop with the brass piano lamp. "I don't ordinarily put items on layaway, young man," Miss Claiborne said. "However, I know your mother, and I believe you when you say you'll have the rest of the money before Christmas, so I'll put the lamp back into storage. Only until Christmas Eve, though. I've noticed other people looking at it."

The boy's next stop was the garage where he had worked a previous summer. "I'm sorry, Antonio," Mr. Weston said. "You're a good worker but I've already hired someone to sweep and keep the place picked up. Good luck, though. I'm sure you'll find something."

At a shop across the highway, the owner looked up from the engine block he was working on. "No, can't say I'm hiring right now. Not that I couldn't use some extra help. But I'm a bit short on money, you know? Got some extra bills I need to clean up. Sorry. Hang in there."

By midday, Antonio had been to more than a dozen stores, shops and garages. They either didn't need any extra help, or already had it. He stood at the edge of the square, kicked at an empty paper cup the wind sent skittering past on the ground, then decided it was time to try the town's handful of restaurants. Two hours later, he had heard several variations on the third reason for being turned down – "13 years old? I'm sorry, we can't hire anyone that young."

So, that was it. He couldn't get the piano lamp. The boy stood at the edge of the highway, his hands in his pockets. Across the way, a dog sniffed around the dumpster next to Weston's Garage. Its ribs showed and it acted hungry. Antonio ran across the highway, a passing truck blaring its horn as he darted past. Mr. Weston came out of the garage as Antonio crouched next to the dog and patted it. "I was hoping you'd come back by, Antonio. Guy I hired last week called in to say he's going out of town with his family. Looks like I can hire you after all."

He reached down and patted the dog on the head. "Don't know where this dog came from. Showed up a couple hours ago and been hanging around since. Skin 'n' bones. Here's a few bucks, kid. Run over and buy some bread or hot dogs or something. Feed this little gal and give her some water. Then you can start cleaning that storeroom back there."

The rest of that day and the following three days, Antonio worked at the garage cleaning, sweeping, stocking and running errands. The church choir was practicing every evening for Christmas service, which meant he had to baby-sit Toya while his mother was at church. Every afternoon after work, he stopped by the antique shop and left what he had earned that day. The morning of Christmas Eve, he was short only $17. Mr. Weston closed the garage at noon and gave the boy his final wages. "I'll see you the 26th, Antonio. I hope you and your mother and sister have a nice Christmas." "Thanks, Mr. Weston. You, too."

Antonio ran the several blocks to the antique shop. "Here's another eight dollars, Miss Claibourne. Can I pay you the rest after Christmas?" The shop owner shook her head as she reached into the cash register and withdrew an envelope containing the money the boy already had given her. "I'm sorry, Antonio, really I am. But I've had other inquiries about the lamp. They're ready to buy it now. I have to be fair to all my customers."

"Yes, ma'am. That's OK." Antonio took the envelope, jammed it in his pocket, and walked out of the shop. Mrs. Claibourne sighed as she reached for the phone.

Antonio took the long way home. He went into several stores but didn't see anything that could match the brass piano lamp. At least he already had bought gifts for his mother and Toya. He would just have to think of some other way to spend the money he had earned for the lamp. Maybe he could buy another dog for Mr. Weston. The garage owner had wanted to keep the little stray but she had disappeared shortly after they fed her.

Marcella and Toya were just sitting down at the supper table when he walked through the door. "Antonio, where have you been?" his mother exclaimed. "We've been worried about you."

But all the boy could do was stare at the old pump organ in the corner of the living room. Perched on the organ above the rack of sheet music was the brass piano lamp.

"Mama, where you get this lamp?" he asked. He walked over to the organ and switched on the brass lamp. It poured a soft glow onto his mother's sheets of Christmas music. Marcella walked in from the kitchen and put her arm around Antonio.

""Isn't it beautiful, son? Sister Thomas brought it over just before supper. She said it was a gift from the church for all the playing I've been doing with the choir and for weddings and funerals and such. She said they wanted to give it to me sooner but the shop owner had it in layaway for a time for another customer. Why, son; what's wrong?"

"Mama, I wanted to give that lamp to you," Antonio blurted out. "It was me who asked Miss Claibourne to hang onto it. I just couldn't get together enough money in time to buy it for you for Christmas." His voice broke and his mother gathered him into her arms.

"Oh, honey, I know you wanted to buy that lamp for me. I know how hard you were working."

He looked up, fighting to hold back his tears. "You knew? How?"

"Oh, you teens aren't the only ones with your networks, you know. We old folks aren't complete fools. Let's just say some Christmas angels let on to me what you were doing. And you know something, son?" She reached into her apron and dabbed at his eyes with a tissue. "As far as I'm concerned, my beautiful lamp is from you just as much as from the church members. You tried so hard to get it. And that means so much to me."

Antonio squirmed as his mother gave him a squeeze. "Mama, I'm hungry!" Toya shouted from the kitchen.

"Supper is getting cold and your sister is getting impatient, Antonio. Let's go eat. After we do the dishes, I'll play the organ and we'll sing some Christmas carols."

# THE CHRISTMAS ROSE

I was just a little tad in knee britches when my pa went off to join General Beauregard and fight the Yankees. My memories from those first half dozen years of my life up to that point include totin' Pa's and Grandpaw's lunch pails to them when they was plantin' cotton and soybeans in the fields that stretched out toward the Loosahatchie bottoms. I remember the fine smells from the kitchen when Grandmaw was cookin' up a batch of cornbread and bacon. I also recollect sittin' on the ground beneath the clean wash wavin' in the breeze, and passin' wooden clothespins up to Ma. Sometimes me and my big sister, Iris, would chase after the chickens when none of the big folks was watchin'.

Most of all, though, what I remember from those years before the war was how Pa showed what a wondrous place this world be. One cold night, he come and fetched me and Iris from our beds in the loft, bundled us up, and carried us out to the barn, where we watched a little calf bein' born. "Look yonder, kids!" he whispered. "A new life comin' into this world. It's a miracle!"

And the summer evenin's sittin' on the front porch with thousands of blinking lights out in the yard and the fields beyond, and he'd tell us they was the lights of tiny lanterns carried by little bitty, flying fairies. Or the time a rainbow soared over the distant hills after a spring rain, and he said to me, "Ain't that beautiful, son? It's a miracle. A message from God remindin' us that there ain't no troubles too heavy for us to tote as long as we let Him into our hearts."

One day when we was carryin' supplies from the wagon into the house, Pa dumped his sack of flour onto the steps and called Iris and me over. He hunkered down onto the ground next to Ma's rose bush and we plopped down alongside him. He told us to take ever so gentle hold of the petals and feel their softness and smell their rich, delicate fragrance. "Flowers this beautiful and lovely; they're a wondrous miracle," he whispered, and smiled at us. Iris with her liking for flowers and plants; she especially liked that.

Then the war come and Pa took up his rifle and a bundle of clothes that Ma put together for him. He hugged me and Iris and Grandpaw and Grandmaw; then Ma and him walked down the steps. They stopped by Ma's rose bush and she picked a rose and give it to Pa and he stuck it in the band of his old slouch hat. Then Pa picked a rose and give it to Ma, and she stuck it into a pocket of her apron. They walked out to the road where a big bunch of men was walkin' by, and he disappeared over the ridge, the whole time wavin' back to us.

We didn't see him no more. I was six years old.

Along about then, the dreams started. We all would get them at different times. Grandpaw would say how he dreamed Pa and him was down at the creek fishin' and they both pulled in some real whoppers. Iris told us how she dreamed Pa was layin' back under a big tree or walkin' through a meadow, the whole time surrounded by beautiful flowers. Grandmaw dreamed it was Pa's and Ma's wedding day again and all the guests was dancin' and carryin' on. My dreams mostly was of Pa whistlin' and laughin' and hoistin' me up high like he did on an evening. Ma's dreams was just a picture and a feelin', she said, of Pa huggin' her ever so tight.

Then Ma took sick just before the Christmas of '64. She been workin' a lot harder to help Grandpaw in the fields, and she kept on the housework with Grandmaw, and it all just seemed to keep whittlin' away at her. That and worryin' about Pa. The week before Christmas, she took to her bed and just stayed there. Grandpaw and Grandmaw took turns sittin' by her. Each day, she seemed smaller than the day before.

Christmas Eve, I kissed Ma goodnight and she smiled at me feeble like. I climbed up to the loft and slipped under the goosedown quilt and drifted off right fast. The last I recall is hearing the mantle clock down in the front room chime 10 times.

When I woke up, the house was all still. Pa was standing at the foot of my bed. He didn't say nothin', just put a finger to his lips and motioned for me to get out of bed and follow him downstairs. I slipped on my pants and pulled my shirt over my head. When I looked again, he was gone. I hustled downstairs and found him standin' next to Ma's bed. Grandmaw was sleepin' in the rocker, bundled into a bedspread that Grandpaw had tucked 'round her.

I'm just an ordinary man," Pa whispered. "I done good things and I done bad. These past few years, I done things that had to be done, and it ain't been easy. What's kept me a'goin' is the love I share with my family." He stopped abruptly and reached down and stroked Ma's hair ever so soft.

He took a few steps back from the bed and looked over at me. "Son, I'm a'goin' to try somethin'. It ain't me that makes it work; it's somethin' a lot bigger, somethin' wondrous. I'm only the tool; the way of getting' it done."

And he commenced to prayin'. I'd heard Pa pray before meals and in church meetin' and kneelin' with Iris and me by our beds, but never like this. His lips moved, but I couldn't hear nothin'. His face was all screwed up real intense. He raised up his hands toward the ceilin' and started tremblin', and tears began runnin' down his cheeks. I just stood there starin'. I began to get powerful afraid when I seen a kinda faint light that seemed to be comin' from Pa that got brighter and brighter. Before long, he was positively glowin' like a bright star, so bright it hurt my eyes. Then he walked over to the bed and reached out again and rested a hand on Ma's forehead.

At first I couldn't tell what was happenin'. Then I saw how Ma was beginnin' to glow but the light within Pa was gettin' fainter. She got brighter and brighter and he got dimmer and dimmer. Before long, she was shinin' like a Christmas star, and Pa was kinda shadowy lookin'. He turned to me and smiled and motioned that we should leave the room.

I followed him out to the porch. Without a word, he walked down the steps, paused to reach down and caressed Ma's rose bush sleepin' there in the winter chill, and walked on out to the lane. He turned and we waved to one another, and then he disappeared into the dark.

I run back inside the house. Grandmaw was leanin' over Ma's bed all excited. Ma was sittin' up and smilin'. I run over to her and she hugged me with the strength she had before. Grandpaw and Iris must have heard us laughin', cause they come runnin' in dressed in their nightshirts, and we all just hugged and laughed and cried. Ma was well again.

Pa come home that spring. He walked with a limp and his face was all sunk in. It'd been four years since we watched him march off to war. Things pretty well settled down to where they been before, although Pa never did seem to be able to work as hard as he done before. I tried talkin' to him 'bout that Christmas night but he just smiled and shook his head and told me, "Some things just be left well enough alone, son. All's well that ends well."

Ever' Christmas since then, somethin' happens to remind us of that special night. On Christmas mornin', no matter how cold or icy the weather be, a single bright red rose blooms on Ma's bush by the porch. Grandpaw says it's a freak of nature. Iris is into books and high-falutin' language and such, and she calls it a "biological phenomenon." All Grandmaw can say is it's the darndest thing she ever seen. Ma and Pa don't say nothin'; they just walk out and smile down at that beautiful flower and hold hands. Me, I know what that rose is. It's a miracle – a Christmas miracle. I done learned to believe in 'em, you know.

# Christmas Call for a Lonely Buckaroo

Shorty paused at the bunkhouse door and glanced back at Angle. The only other hired hand on the ranch this Christmas Eve was lounging in his bunk reading a five-year-old Popular Mechanics by the light of a coal oil lantern as he idly twirled his key chain with the plastic-encased four leaf clover.

"Say, Angle; why don'tcha come on into town with me to this here Christmas pageant the kids is puttin' on at the school? Beats hangin' around here all by your lonesome."

Angle let the magazine drop on his chest and sighed. "I appreciate the offer, Shorty; I truly do. I'd feel funny goin', though. Bein' new in these parts and not knowin' anyone. I'd just be an outsider makin' people uncomfortable. No, I just better stay here."

Shorty hung his hat back on the hook and folded his arms. "My mind is made up, Angle. You're goin'. It'll do ya good."

Angle looked over at his friend and frowned. Why anyone who had to duck his head any time he went through a doorway should have the nickname Shorty, he didn't know. But he had worked here long enough to recognize the look in Shorty's eye and understand that crossed arm gesture. He sighed and reached under his bunk for his boots.

The light from the five-room schoolhouse made the snow glisten outside the windows. Shorty and Angle tied their horses in the grove alongside the other horses, slogged past the rows of pickups and cars, and joined the muffled procession of frost-breathed figures hustling into the foyer of the building. Shorty exchanged greetings with neighbors as they stomped the snow off their feet and hung their coats, hats and scarves. Angle stumbled through his comments as Shorty introduced him through the crowd.

They edged past several people and sat down in a row of folding metal chairs toward the back of the room just as shepherds and sheep wearing old pajamas and bathrobe costumes trooped onto the makeshift stage. The pianist started tapping out a slightly off-key "Angels We Have Heard on High."

Partway through the first act, a toddler in front of the two cowboys began fidgeting in her seat. Her mother leaned over, hugged the child and kissed her on the head. The child sat still for a while but began squirming again. Again the mother leaned over, whispering in her ear. The girl was still for several minutes but then began fidgeting once more. Shorty noticed Angle shift forward and whisper something in the girl's ear. The girl turned around and smiled at him as he eased back in his seat. She looked up at her mother, who smiled down at her, then turned and looked back briefly at Angle. In the front of the school, The Three Wise Men stumbled through their lines.

During the intermission, Shorty and Angle joined the hot cider line in the school's vestibule. Ahead of them, a girl gave the teacher a nickel and accepted her steaming cup. As she stood off to the side to sip it, a heavyset man with a thick neck bulging out of his three-piece suit came stomping in from outside. He removed his homburg and fur coat, snorted, and looked down at the girl.

"Well, now, little lady, where did you get those big ears?" he said in a booming voice.

Shorty's head whipped around but Angle had already darted over to the girl's side. He crouched down next to her, saw the tears welling up in her eyes, and his glare whipped up at the man looming overhead.

"She got them ears the same place she got her purty hair and her sweet eyes and her gentle smile. Where the hell you get your manners?"

The crowd around them immediately hushed and stared. A woman who had started to make her way through the crowd stopped and watched too. The large man snorted, turned, and stalked into the classroom. Angle pulled his kerchief from around his neck and dabbed at the girl's eyes.

"Young lady, I apologize for my rough language," he said. "A dumb ol' cowpoke like me. Heck, you oughta hear how I talk to my mule and the coyotes."

The girl smiled and shrugged. "That's OK. My daddy would say a naughty word if he hit his thumb with a hammer or Old Thunder didn't want to be saddled."

Angle patted her on the shoulder and joined Shorty for the program's last act. Toward the end of the act, an angel in a bedsheet robe and window curtain wings in wire frames froze as he began to speak his lines. The teacher prompting the children from the side of the room hissed, "And the shepherds returned…!" In the crowd, you could have heard a saddle creak.

Suddenly, from the back of the room, came a crashing sound. In an instant, all attention had shifted from the stage-struck angel to the last row of chairs, where Shorty was helping Angle up off the floor.

"Dang, Angle; you OK?" he whispered.

"Ain't no horse throwed me yet but I couldn't get back up and on," was the reply.

Faces turned back to the front of the room where the angel, his nervousness broken by the collapsing chair, began speaking his lines in a soft but confident voice. "And the shepherds returned, glorifying and praising God for all the things that they had heard and seen, as it was told unto them."

The rest of the angels and shepherds began singing, joined by the animals in the stable. The play had come to a successful conclusion.

Snow began falling again as Shorty and Angle rode through the fields back to the ranch. Angle pulled out his keychain and began idly twirling it. Shorty looked over and said, "Where's your lucky clover?"

"My what?"

"Your lucky four-leaf clover. That one in a plastic ring you got on the end of your key chain."

Angle rode on for a while before shrugging and replying, "I give it away."

"Give it away? To who?"

"That little gal who was fidgetin'. She needed a play thing. Now it'll be lucky for her."

"Well, I'll be…."

They had dismounted and were walking their horses into the stable when Shorty said, "You know that big bruiser. The one you give what for to?"

"Yeah, what about 'im?"

"He ain't just big in size. He's big around town. Hot shot lawyer, on the county board of commissioners, trustee on the bank board."

Angle laughed. "Mebbe I oughta get my lucky four leaf clover back." He tossed the saddle up on the stall wall. "Shoot, Shorty; the bigger they are, the more fun it is to light into 'em. Makes things interesting."

Back in the bunkhouse, Shorty crawled under the covers in his bunk as Angle settled down in his bunk with the Popular Mechanics. Before he drifted off, Shorty mumbled, "Hey, Angle."

"Yeah."

"You done it a'purpose, didn't you?"

"Done what?"

"Fell off your chair. I seen you kinda kick at the leg and make it collapse. You took that spill on purpose."

"Well," Angle replied. "That little fella up there not rememberin' his lines, that's a rough thing. I been there. I wanted to do somethin' to kinda break the tension. Fallin' oughta my chair was the only thing I could think of. Worked though, didn't it?"

"Yeah, I guess so," Shorty said, his voice heavy with sleep. "Funny thing, though."

"Yeah, what's that?"

"That little girl in front of us, and the one in the cider line, and the boy on the stage; they're all kids of Mrs. Willowby; widow woman whose husband was at the wrong end of a herd when it stampeded a couple years ago. The bigger of the two girls is Jodie. She's eight. And the little one, Phyllis; she's three. And Andrew is five years old."

"Well, I'll be." Those were the last words spoken in the bunkhouse that night.

The next morning Shorty banged through the door with an armload of firewood. Angle was standing by the phone with a stunned look on his face.

"What's up, buckaroo?"

"That was that Mrs. Willowby – Meredith Willowby. She said she seen what I done for Phyllis and Jodie and figured out what I done for Andrew. Said she really appreciated it and wants me to come over for Christmas dinner."

"Pard, that's just fine. You go on ahead; I'll be able to look after things here today."

"But you had plans."

"With friends, yeah, but they'll understand and I can see 'em anytime. You go on ahead now.

So that's the way it was, with Angle saddling up again and promising to call Shorty later in the day.

The sun was glowing out from a high horizon when the phone rang. Shorty could hardly understand what Angle was saying because of all the laughing and giggling and music in the background. They finally managed to exchange "Merry Christmas!" to one another and Angle hung up.

Shorty opened the bunkhouse door and lit a cigarette. Slump, the old watch hound, came out from his doghouse and stretched. Shorty smiled down at the dog. "You know, Slump, I've known women that I could feel envy for their boyfriends and pity for their husbands. But that Willowby gal; she's the sort of filly a man could envy either her boyfriend or her husband. Looks like things could work out pretty good for Angle and her, and for those three little kids."

He looked out over the snow-blanketed buildings and trees and said quietly, "Merry Christmas, Angle." He lifted his face to the setting sun and felt the mix of clean fresh air and warm light on his face and said in an even quieter voice, "Happy Birthday, Jesus. And thanks for everything."

He turned, walked into the bunkhouse and shut the door. Old Slump yawned and crawled back into his house. Snow began falling again, and the hushed sound was like a million tiny bells ringing their timeless message of faith and good will.

# THE CARPENTER WHO LOVED CHILDREN

*(Count me among those many people who are annoyed by how the true meaning of Christmas – the celebration of the birthday of Jesus Christ -- has been largely hijacked by a mind-boggling emphasis on crass commercialism. This story is my effort to give appropriate recognition to one of the nicer aspects of contemporary holiday tradition – Santa Claus – while making the jolly old man subservient to the birth of the son of God.)*

Once upon a time, many years ago and in another country far away, two men in a small town had a carpenter shop. Both were skilled in working with wood but in their habits they were very different. One worked long hours every day to turn out finely crafted furniture and farm implements. The other carpenter worked irregular hours. Sometimes he toiled late into the night by the light of his lantern and slept until lunch the following day. He preferred sitting under a tree by the town well crafting tops and dolls and little wagons for the children. He would often disappear for days at a time with nothing but a bag slung over his shoulder.

In appearance too, the men differed. The one was of average build with powerful muscles developed from hard honest work. The other was almost as wide as he was tall.

Despite these differences, the two were best of friends. When townspeople asked the dependable carpenter why he tolerated his partner's behavior, Joseph replied, "Nicholas is a good man. He chooses to place his priorities elsewhere. When he works, he is as fine a carpenter as I. When he does not work, he is a friend to the children. What fault lies in this?"

One day Joseph married a lovely maiden named Mary. Nicholas was in awe of his friend's wife. Whereas many townspeople looked down on Nicholas for his erratic ways, Mary was kind to him and always had a warm word for him. When he learned she was going to have a baby, he was beside himself with happiness for his two friends. He immediately began making a cradle for the infant, selecting only the finest woods and working with the utmost detail and precision.

But Nicholas' old ways of wandering began to creep back into daily routine. Months passed but the cradle was not yet completed when Joseph told him that he and Mary must leave Nazareth for a short time for the census decreed by the ruling king. The two men shook hands and embraced, and Nicholas helped his friend place Mary, who was now close to conceiving, on the back of the donkey who would carry her to Bethlehem.

Several nights later, Nicholas completed the cradle and fell asleep on a pile of sawdust by the workbench. He was awakened by a voice that seemed to come from nowhere and everywhere. "Your friends are in danger." Nicholas was frightened. He knew the kind words of Mary and the friendly tone of Joseph and the critical comments of the townspeople and the cheerful laughter of the children. This was a voice he did not recognize. Convinced, though, that Joseph and Mary needed him, he gathered together his cloak, a flask of water and a loaf of bread, tied the cradle to his back, took up his staff, and set out at a brisk pace on the road to Bethlehem.

It was an arduous journey but one night he finally stood on a hill overlooking the plain that was his journey's end. High in the sky in the distance a star brighter than he ever seen before shone down over the countryside. He hurried on, for the road was rocky and winding, and he still had a great distance to travel.

Nicholas finally arrived in Bethlehem and began inquiring for Mary and Joseph at the town's inns. Finally, one innkeeper jerked a hand toward the back of his inn. "We had no room because of those who are here for the census so I offered them a place in my stable," he said in a gruff voice.

Nicholas hurried around to the back. When he pushed open the double doors, the warm scent and gentle lowing of cattle, a softly nickering horse and a few chickens pecking about greeted him. Two cats peered down at him from the loft and a litter of puppies peeped out from under the bottom board of a stall.

Easing down the cradle, Nicholas rubbed his aching neck and looked about. He felt his gaze pulled toward a manger filled with hay. In the center of the hay was a depressed area on which lay a piece of paper. He picked up the paper and read, "Gentle friend, we knew you would come. We have fled to Egypt for the sake of our newborn child. Please return to the shop and keep it until our return. Continue to be kind to the children. They enjoy your toys so. P.S. It is a boy child. We have named him Jesus."

Nicholas read the words and wept with joy for Joseph and Mary and their newborn child. Then he thought of how his friends were in some sort of danger, and his tears became those of sadness and frustration.

"I should have been here to help you," he moaned, "but I let you down."

He folded the note and slipped it in his robe, took up the cradle, and walked from the warmth of the stable into the bitter cold air and the long journey back to Nazareth.

In a mountain pass by the bank of a stream, Nicholas slumped down against a boulder to rest for a short time. He was awakened by screams and shouting. Scrambling to his feet, he saw a woman running toward him clutching a baby in her arms. Racing after her was a roughly-dressed group of men armed with daggers and clubs.

When she saw a fellow traveler rise up from the ground by the bridge, the woman cried, "Help us, good stranger! Please help us!"

She ducked around Nicholas, holding her child tightly to her. The bandits slowed for a moment when they saw the size of the man facing them, and then rushed forward. The mother ran to the far end of the bridge. Thoughts of smiling children and toys and Mary and Joseph and their newborn child flashed through the mind of Nicholas. He reached down, swung up the cradle he had brought too late for the child Jesus, and with the roar of a lion defending its young, rushed at the attackers, swinging the cradle like a giant club.

His strength was great and his anger greater but he was one against five. The mother and her child watched as Nicholas, with one final swing of the now shattered cradle, smashed down the only brigand left standing just as the man thrust his knife into the carpenter's side, adding one final wound to the many Nicholas already bore. He collapsed to the ground among those he had already struck down.

The mother ran back across the bridge and knelt next to Nicholas. He fumbled weakly in his robe and pulled forth a piece of paper he held tightly in one fist. He reached with his other hand toward a pouch tied to the waist of his robe and pulled out a small wooden bird. He pushed it toward her, whispered "For your child," and his head fell to one side. The woman took the toy from his hand, leaned over and kissed his forehead. Realizing she could do nothing more for him, she gathered up her infant and hurried on. Behind, the wind whistled through the pass over the pile of motionless bodies sprawled at the edge of the bridge.

When Nicholas' eyes opened, he was back in his workshop. Or so he thought. Sitting up, he saw the shop was much larger than the one he shared with his friend Joseph. Looking out a window, he was dazzled by a white landscape that sparkled in the sun. Nor was that all. Perched on tabletops, sitting cross-legged on the floor, gazing down from rafters, were a multitude of little people dressed in red and green trousers, tunics and hats.

From one of the windows streaming in sunshine came a voice similar to, but younger than, the voice Nicholas had heard in the dream warning him his friends needed him.

"You were there for them and for me," the voice said.

Nicholas was surprised to discover he wasn't scared. Nevertheless, he was puzzled.

"I was too late," he said. "They had to flee, the three of them."

"They fled," the voice agreed, "but you then saved the life of another infant and its mother. Inasmuch as you came to the aid of one of the smallest of these, my brethren, you aided me.

"The faces about you are those children through the ages who have died a death too sudden, sad and premature. They now abide here with you, and with their help you shall fulfill your life's dream. You enjoyed roaming

23

the countryside near Nazareth giving toys to the children. You now have helpers to assist you in creating toys. Every year from this day hence, you will deliver those toys to the children of the world to help commemorate the anniversary of my birth."

Nicholas felt a renewed strength and happiness glow within him. He looked about and smiled at his many toyshop helpers, and they smiled back at him.

"Bring joy to the children, Saint Nicholas," the voice said. Happy shouts of "Santa Claus!" echoed throughout the warm, cheery workshop.

Thus did Santa Claus come to be many years ago. Throughout the centuries, he has come to be known by different names in different lands. Some wonder how he is able to do so much and travel so far in such little time. Santa does have helpers since he can do only so much. Senior elves who bear an amazing resemblance to the kindly old man sometimes take his place for appearances before Christmas. Occasionally he recruits someone locally to fill in for him and his legions of elves.

Every so often, though, a child tiptoes downstairs on Christmas night, peeks around the corner in the dark and quiet house, and sees a large white-bearded man with a red hat and suit. The child watches as the man places presents about. Before he disappears up the chimney or out the window, if the house has a Nativity scene, the man kneels before it and prays. If he listens carefully, the child might hear the man whisper, "Thank you for giving me another chance to bring happiness to the children." And the child hears a voice from nowhere and everywhere reply, "And thank you, kind and faithful servant."

# The Shepherd and the Centurion

*(This story began forming in my mind while I was among several hundred townfolk crowded into the county courthouse a week before Christmas, listening to a chorus sing Christmas carols. As I sat on the floor in the crowded lobby and listened to the words and the music, I pulled out my pocket notebook and jotted down notes that became the outline for this story.)*

It's been almost 2,000 years. The sheepherders and other nomads still speak of the legend of the shepherd and the centurion. As the desert winds howl past their campfires and they watch over their flocks and listen for sounds in the darkness, they tell the story of that special night and its effect on two very different men.

The shepherd's name was Jude. He had been tending flocks for more than threescore years. He was a quiet man and his knowledge of sheep was marked by a timidity that resulted in his being given little respect despite his years of experience.

The centurion's name was Barnabas. He was one of the emperor's youngest centurions, having been accorded this honor due to the ferocity and lust for killing he exhibited in battle against Rome's enemies. He was a confident, even haughty, individual.

On this day in early winter, Jude had driven his flock to an oasis he knew to have water clear and plentiful. As the sheep drank, he stood vigilant on a slight rise nearby, shivering in his cloak while leaning on his shepherd's crook. He stood upright when he saw a horseman galloping toward him.

It was Barnabas, traveling to his new command. Seeing the sheep clustered around the water, he spurred his horse forward, scattering the bleating animals. Jude shrank from the stranger as he scurried to round up the frightened beasts.

"Old man! Keep your charges back while my horse and I drink!" Barnabas laughed as he dismounted and removed his helmet. "A soldier of the emperor does not take second place to a sheepherder and his four-legged geese."

Jude bowed low and muttered apologies as he brought the flock under control.

"A thousand pardons," he said softly. "Pray thee, drink thy fill, and we shall await our turn."

Barnabas snorted and tossed back his cloak as he knelt to drink alongside his steed. He remounted and, ignoring the sheep clustering near the water, spurred his horse to a gallop and sped off over the dunes. Jude ushered his sheep back down to the water and sighed as they began drinking again.

That evening, Jude had joined up with other sheepherders. Their flocks together, the men gathered by their fires while guarding over the combined herds. Suddenly the sheep began moving restlessly and bleating. Those shepherds on watch and those gathered by the fire stared upward and cringed as the night sky suddenly brightened, and shining overhead appeared a shimmering figure of an angel.

"Fear not," the angel's words rolled down. "For, behold, I bring you good tidings of great joy, which shall be to all people. For unto you is born this day in the city of David a Savior, which is Christ the Lord. And this shall be a sign unto you; ye shall find the babe wrapped in swaddling clothes, lying in a manger."

The light grew brighter still and shepherds and sheep alike huddled together as a multitude of angels appeared, saying, "Glory to God in the highest, and on earth peace, good will toward men."

As suddenly as the apparition had appeared, so did it fade from view and leave nothing but the dark, cold December sky.

The shepherds gathered and talked excitedly about what they had just witnessed. It was decided they would travel the short distance to Bethlehem, which lay a short distance away, to see this wondrous new king that had been described to them. One shepherd must of necessity stay behind to guard the sheep and chosen for that lonely duty was Jude. His heart yearned to go with the others but he had little courage to speak his mind.

Some miles away on that same night, the centurion had eased his horse to a trot. Ahead he spied a road. The light of the moon showed him several objects scattered along behind large boulders that lined the road at that point. His military intuition caused the centurion to rein in his horse and study what he saw more carefully. It was a handful of man roughly dressed, armed with daggers and spears. Slipping off his horse and drawing his sword, he crept forward.

From around a bend in the road came three men on camels, moving at a brisk gait. As this small band came parallel to the boulders, the outlaws – which the centurion now understood the men waiting in ambush to be – sprang forward, shouting. Instinctively, Barnabas also shouted, a mighty war cry that had precluded the death of many an enemy of Rome. The men turned to see this apparition, his cloak flying and his sword raised high, dashing at them.

The bandits froze as this figure that had meant death to so many others came at them. He was about to lash out at the cowering figures when he froze. The bandits and the three men on camels stared at Barnabas, then followed his stare upward. There in the sky, one star stood out from the others, glowing with great intensity.

The centurion lowered his sword and pointed it at the group of bandits.

"Go," he snarled. "Leave this place."

Sensing their lives had somehow been spared by a foe who was greater than all their number, the bandits turned and fled into the night. Barnabas sheathed his sword and strode toward the three men on camels. Their garments, he saw, were rich and heavy.

"Who art thou and where goest thou?" he asked.

"We come from lands to the East. We take gifts to a king who has been foretold by the stars and the planets," answered one in a heavy accent. "He must truly be a mighty figure and we come to pay homage. Will you come with us, brave stranger?"

Barnabas hesitated.

"No," he finally answered as he turned back toward his waiting horse. "I know not what has happened here and it leaves me with strange feelings I do not remember experiencing before. I have another destination."

The three strangers bid him farewell and turned back onto the road toward the king who awaited them.

Some miles distant, Jude stood by his flock, still wondering over the sight the shepherds had witnessed earlier. Bleating from the flock interrupted his thoughts. Running forward, he saw the sheep milling toward him, pursued by low, four-legged shadows – a pack of jackals.

Jude felt a great fear and turned to run but something drew his gaze skyward. Looking up, he saw a star that, alone among the others in the night sky, glowed with great intensity. As sheep raced past him, he turned toward the jackals, roared like a lion, and hurled himself at them, his staff raised high. The beasts, seeing and hearing this threat, turned and fled. Jude watched them go, wondered at what had happened, then turned his attention to the sheep to control and calm them.

It was midday the following day before the other shepherds returned. They related to Jude what they had witnessed. They had come upon a baby lying in a manger in a stable, tended to by his parents and also by three strangers on camels. Various beasts in the poor building gathered about, adding their gentle gaze and warm breath to a scene that was humble yet majestic.

The sun was lowering into the western sky when Jude explained he would return on the morrow, then started toward the nearby town to see this wonder for himself. Following the directions his fellow shepherds had provided, he soon found himself at the entrance to the stable. He was about to step inside when he heard a footstep next to him. It was the centurion who had mocked him at the oasis.

Barnabas removed his helmet and smiled at Jude.

"We meet again, shepherd," he said in a voice much gentler than that he had used the day before.

The two entered into the hay-filled warmth of the structure. A man stepped from the shadows and stood by a woman kneeling next to a manger. They nodded to the two strangers.

"Welcome, my friends," the man said.

Jude and Barnabas walked forward and looked down at the infant lying in the manger.

"I have the same feeling … " began Jude.

" … as when the star shone down upon me," finished Barnabas.

"As when the star shown down upon the two of you," the man said gently.

"Upon all of us," the woman said in a musical voice.

Barnabas looked at the woman with question in his eyes as he knelt by the manger and reached toward the babe. She gently lifted the infant and placed Him in the centurion's arms. Barnabas felt a strength greater than had ever come from sword or dagger or the might of all the soldiers under his command. He leaned down, gently kissed the child on the forehead, then turned toward Jude. The shepherd too was kneeling. He reached out and took the child into his arms. He felt a gentleness greater than he had ever felt before from the littlest lamb. Jude too bent down, kissed the child on the forehead, and returned Him to his mother's care.

The shepherd and the centurion stood, bowed to the family before them, and backed out into the evening air. Jude took up his crook. Barnabas placed his helmet back on his head. Leaping aboard his horse, he wheeled it around and saluted down toward the shepherd. Jude raised his staff in a return salute to the centurion, who galloped down the alleyway and disappeared.

Jude returned to his flocks. In the years that followed, fellow shepherds wondered at the energy and determination he exhibited – characteristics of strength they would have expected in a much younger man. He took his place at the campfires as a leader, and was greatly respected and his advice carefully followed. To the day he died, no sheep in his care was ever lost.

As for Barnabas, that brightest and most promising of the emperor's centurions was never heard of again. Stories did come from the far reaches of the land of a man dressed in the clothes of a soldier who fought not for an emperor or an empire. A traveler who was thirsty and starving was given food and water. A maiden was rescued from a gang bent on kidnap and worse. A family fighting against a flash flood was pulled to safety. A gang of marauders was driven from a caravan it was attacking. In every case, the stranger seemed to materialize from nowhere, provided what aid was necessary, then disappeared as quickly as he had appeared.

One story that traveled among the campfires told of a boy on his way to market who came upon a man in the ripped and worn armor of a centurion. The man was kneeling in prayer before a sword and a dagger formed into a makeshift cross.

# THE ANIMALS' CHRISTMAS GIFT

*(According to legend, animals are given the ability to speak on the night before Christmas. How might they use such a gift? That's the premise for the following story -- that, and a comment one time from my oldest sister that children, thank God, tend to be resilient.)*

Frank had peeked enough at the packages under the tree during the first 24 days of December to guess which were his.

It gave him a warm feeling to know the Kinkaids treated him as one of their own. Still, as the eight-year old gazed out his bedroom window at the snow gleaming in the moonlight, he couldn't help thinking about his family – his mother's kisses, his father's hugs, playing and laughing with his big sister and little brother.

His breath on the cold glass made it fog over and blurred the landscape below. Visions of love and laughter were pushed aside by images of the empty beer bottles, piles of unwashed clothes, fist-sized holes in the walls, a door kicked off its hinges and, finally, the beatings and screaming, the hiding space under the bed, and the police cars in the driveway.

The woman from the agency had told him Suzie was in a special home and Keith was still in the hospital. When he had asked where his parents were, she kept changing the subject.

So, here he was. He wished it were already Christmas morning so he could open his presents. Something was missing, though, and it dawned on him that he had nothing for the family who had taken him in.

"Psst! Hey, kid!"

Frank's head jerked around. He was alone in the room.

"Hey, you up there!"

He stared down at the lawn below the window. Craning her neck toward him was the family duck, Shirley.

"Get your shoes on, grab your coat and hustle down here, kid! We gotta work fast!"

An adult might have reacted with shock or disbelief. Such is the faith of children that Frank didn't hesitate. Four minutes later, he was outside and crouched down next to Shirley.

"Why can you talk? How do you do that?"

"No time no time no time!" she fussed back at him. "Got work to do got work to do! Follow me follow me!" And with that, she turned and waddled toward the barn. Frank followed.

From the doghouse by the back door ambled Bubba, the family Labrador retriever. He stretched, yawned, and asked the passing duck and boy, "Is it Christmas already? I clean forgot. I was dreaming about steak bones."

He trotted alongside Frank. "Steak drippings are OK but give me a good steak bone any day."

A sleek black shadow popped out from the carpet-lined box on the back porch, flowed down the stairs and galloped up to the passing parade. It was Herbert, the family cat.

He rubbed up against Frank's leg and the boy reached down to scratch the cat's ears.

"Merry Christmas, boy," he purred. "Don't worry. We're here to help you."

The duck waited impatiently by the barn door. Frank pushed it open and the quartet squeezed into the warm interior that smelled of hay, old leather and wood.

The oldest of the small flock of chickens came up to the boy.

"Frank, it's a cold night for such a young boy to be out," Debbie clucked. "Here, now. You come sit yourself in this hay.'"

Frank sank into the pile of fragrant hay. The chickens snuggled in close while Bubba and Herbert sat nearby. Shirley quacked out, "Here we are here we are here we are!"

"My goodness, Shirley; calm yourself," lowed a quiet voice. Frieda, the family cow, ambled from the shadows. "We have plenty of time. Don't fret yourself into a dither, dear."

Frank looked up and smiled at the brown and white bovine looming over him. A gentle nickering came from an adjacent stall. A reddish brown quarter horse emerged to stand beside the cow.

"Well now, Frieda," neighed Gordon; "I do believe we're ready to start."

"Not quite not quite not quite" sputtered Shirley. "Where's Charles? Where's Charles?" The duck waddled to another stall. A moment later, amid a flurry of quacking and baaing, Charles, the family goat, came trotting out with the duck pecking at his legs.

"A body can't even get a good night's sleep around here with all this fussing," Charles grumbled. "Can't it wait 'til morning?" But he sank down to the barn floor next to Gordon and chewed his cud quietly, waiting.

"All right then, let's get started," Frieda said. "Frank, we know you miss your family and we're sorry. Life is neither easy nor fair. All we can do is make the best of things. Now you wish you had something to give the Kinkaids for their kindness in letting you stay with them until, God willing, your family can be together again. All of us" – and she nodded to the circle of animals around the boy – "are here to help you give in return to those who have given to you."

"But I don't have any money," Frank said. "And it's almost Christmas morning."

Herbert stood and rubbed against Frank. "Life's richest gifts come from the heart," the cat meowed, "not from the pocketbook."

"Why, sure," Bubba woofed. "We'll lick this little problem cleaner than a steak bone."

"Of course, dear," clucked Debbie, ruffling her feathers. "Where there's a will, there's a way."

Thus began the busiest Christmas night of the young boy's life.

The following morning, a pile of torn wrapping paper filled the center of a living room resounding with chatter and laughter.

"Frank," Mrs. Kinkaid said, "we're so happy to have you with us this Christmas Day."

The boy looked up from the toys surrounding him. He scrambled to his feet, said "I'll be right back!" and ran out the front door. He came back in with an armful of packages and began handing them to the open-mouthed family.

"Frank, where on earth?" began Mr. Kinkaid but Grandfather Kinkaid cleared his throat and looked at his son. "I mean, what on earth could this be?" Jim Kinkaid tore open his package and gave a long whistle at the gleaming pair of longhorn steer horns – horns that had belonged to Frieda's great-grandfather and for which she had led Frank to their hiding place in a distant grove of trees in the upper pasture.

"These will make a great gun rack! Thank you, Frank."

Virginia Kinkaid was exclaiming over the clump of bright orange and red berries clustered in shiny green leaves. "Where on earth did you find this bittersweet, dear? What a wonderful addition to my next flower arrangement!"

Frank beamed as he recalled following the quacking Shirley through the woods to the vines she had spotted some days earlier.

"Land sakes alive! My old high school baseball!" shouted Grandfather Kinkaid. "I've been looking everywhere for this for nigh onto 10 years now! Frank, how in heaven's name …"

And Frank smiled at the image of Bubba trotting up to him, fresh dirt on the old dog's muzzle and front paws, and the baseball held gingerly in his mouth.

Grandmother Kinkaid was gently stroking the cluster of peacock feathers she had unwrapped. "Won't these look fine in the wall display I'm making for the nursing home," she murmured. "See how they shimmer in the light. God bless you, Frank."

The boy said a silent thanks to Herbert for leading him to where the cat had found the feathers during one of his many nocturnal wonderings.

"Oh, Frank, thank you so much!" Little Jamie was gingerly holding three baby chicks to her face. "They're so soft and cuddly."

"We'll fix up a box for them," Mrs. Kinkaid said. "They're just babies, honey, and you need to be careful with them. Frank, what a sweet gift. Wherever did you find them?"

Frank just smiled as he thought of Debbie leading him to her nestful of chicks tucked away in a far corner of the barn.

"Look, everybody, at what Frank wrapped our presents in," said Grandfather Kinkaid. "Old feed sacks. By golly, with this red and green Co-op emblem and black lettering, they're darned attractive. Frank, that was right clever of you to think of using sacks for wrapping paper.

Frank thought of how Charles the goat had solved the problem of wrapping paper by grumbling and fussing as he led Frank to his secret cache of feed sacks he enjoyed resting on.

"Frank, where's my gift?" piped up little Miles. Frank stood, took the five-year old by the hand, and led him to the front door.

"You don't have to be scared of horses anymore, Miles," Frank said. He pointed out to the yard where Gordon stood. The whole family watched with mouths open as the horse knelt down, turned his handsome head toward the house, and neighed loudly.

"I had a talk with him," Frank said, "and he promised you can ride him anytime you want and he'll be super gentle."

Later that afternoon, Frank led Gordon by his lead around the yard. Miles clung to the saddle, laughing and giggling. As they passed between the barn and the house, the other animals watched without a sound, for Christmas night had passed.

Frank thought about that night and his scattered family, and felt sad. Then he heard the tap on the kitchen window, waved back at the elderly man and woman waving to him, thought of the hope of Christmases and better days to come, and felt better.

He felt a nudge on his shoulder. Gordon pushed up his muzzle against Frank and the boy was sure he saw the horse wink at him.

35

# A CHRISTMAS TRINITY

The old man, the girl and the dog were a common sight around the old river town.

Every day they made their way along the plank sidewalks among the townspeople and over the dirt roads among horse-drawn wagons. The blind old man was always flanked by the mute girl in her torn smock and the dog with its rough coat and stub of a tail. For some townspeople, the trio was an opportunity to call out a clever insult. Most people in the town, though, responded to the daily walks of the three with a spare coin, a leftover half loaf of bread, a few slices of ham, an apple or two, or perhaps a secondhand pair of gloves or threadbare coat.

These offerings were sufficient for the three companions to survive in rough but tolerable fashion. For shelter, they lived in an abandoned switchman's shanty at the edge of the railroad yard on the outskirts of town. They heated the clapboard building in the winter with lumps of coal scavenged from the trackbeds over which steam locomotives chugged past.

No one thought much to wonder where each had come from or how he or she had come to band together. They were an accepted part of the town's daily life.

A curious mind pursuing the matter might have learned that the old man had come to town years before as a farmboy from some nameless settlement, drawn by the city lights. He had found employment in a local factory but a blast of flame from a furnace had cost him his sight and his ability to pay for the room he had been renting. He had settled in the switchman's shanty and used his familiarity with the town layout that his too-short years of sight had provided to establish a regular begging route.

The curious mind could have learned that the mother of the little girl was, to use a term used back then, "a fallen woman." The girl's father could have been any of a number of men who came knocking late at night at the door of the rowhouse where the woman lived. She died shortly after giving birth. During the little girl's first five years, she was shunted from one home to another. She never did talk much. By the time her final family moved away and left her behind, she had become mute. When the blind old man took her in, he became her voice and she became his eyes.

Further investigation could have revealed that the dog had been one of a litter born under the loading dock of a warehouse. Its mother was a nondescript stray and, as with the little girl, the father was uncertain. Half the litter had died shortly after birth and the dog was the other half's only survivor. One ear was half gone, the other nearly torn in two, his neck and chest were covered with scars, and his tail was just a stub, the result of several mischievous boys wielding a sharp butcher knife. Though gray whiskers were evident on his muzzle, he still exhibited a strength, street savvy and alertness that had caused him to become a loyal guardian for his two companions in exchange for food and shelter.

So the years passed, and so this trio wove a borderline but tolerable existence in the fiber of the town.

One night in early winter, a cold breeze muttered through the pieces of cardboard and scrap wood that chinked the cracks in the shanty's walls. The old man told the little girl to go knock at the backdoor of a boarding house. The owner could be trusted, though with some grumbling, to have some leftover soup from the evening meal that would suffice for supper for the three of them.

Leaving the dog to watch the old man, the girl wrapped her patched cloak about her and set out. She was several blocks from her destination when, through the rising wind, she heard the sound of singing. It was coming from one of the larger churches in town. She and her companions had often slipped into the church when no one was around, seeking a cool sanctuary on a hot day or a place to momentarily escape the cold of winter while making their rounds. The little girl eased through a delivery door in an adjacent building, walked down a short dark hallway, then peeped through a door.

The church glowed with candles everywhere. The aromatic scent of pine and cedar wafted from evergreens and garlands decorating the benches, walls and windows. The girl stood with her mouth open as she listened to the townspeople who filled the church sing one beautiful song after another. The songs sounded familiar. She thought they were songs the people sang once a year, though why they sang such beautiful songs so infrequently, she didn't understand.

The walk had tired her, and the warmth and songs were soothing. She sank to the floor, closed her eyes, and let her mind float among the beauty that was in the church within. To the sound of choruses and harmony, she soon fell asleep.

When the little girl awakened, all was quiet. Scrambling to her feet, she peeked into the church. It was empty, though the rich scent of evergreens lingered and a few candles still flickered. She eased through the door and walked toward the front of the church, taking in the hushed beauty of this sacred place. Reaching the front, she saw a group of statues. Shepherds and three men dressed in robes stood and knelt in front of a lean-to made of straw and rough lumber. Going closer, she saw sheep, several donkeys, a horse and a cow, and three strange animals with funny heads and humps on their backs.

All of these statues were gathered in a circle. In the center were a man and woman dressed in robes simpler than those of the three men. The man and woman knelt next to a manger and in the manger was a little baby, only barely covered with a white cloth. The girl instinctively reached out and spread the cloth so the baby would be warmer.

When she touched the baby, from deep within, some distant knowledge and far-away experiences meshed together. Kneeling down next to the manger, the little girl reached out a hand and touched one arm of the baby. Uttering the first words she had spoken in years, she sang in a soft, shaky voice, "Happy birthday to you; happy birthday to you; happy birthday, dear Jesus; happy birthday to you."

She leaned forward and kissed the baby on the forehead. It suddenly dawned on her that an outcast such as she did not belong here. Turning, she ran down the aisle, through the door, down the dark hall, and back out into the night.

In the almost two hours she had been in the church, the winds had brought a blizzard howling through the region. Snowflakes whipped by the winds poured from the sky as the little girl wrapped her cloak more tightly about her and set out for the boardinghouse. She had gone only a short distance before she realized she was lost in the whirling white. She turned and started for home but each step became slower then the one before as the wind and cold beat down on her.

Back in the switchman's shanty, the old man was worried when the little girl didn't return. Rousing the dog, he cracked open the door and, feeling the onslaught of the storm, bade the animal seek out the girl and bring her home safely. The ever-faithful dog slipped through the door and was gone in an instant, bounding through the snow toward the direction the girl had gone.

By the time the dog found the little girl, she was a white-covered mound in the snow. Whining, he lay beside her and licked her cold face. She gave a faint smile, wrapped an arm around his neck, and huddled close to the warmth of his body. He whined and licked at her face again but she didn't move. Sighing, he instinctively wedged his body closer to that of his companion. The snow continued to fall and soon the two friends became one indistinguishable mound under the snow.

Back in the shanty, the old man fell asleep waiting for their return.

*The little girl opened her eyes. A warmth flowed through her. Looking up, she saw the kindest face she had ever seen gazing down at her. A man with long hair and a beard, and wearing a shimmering white robe, held her in his arms.*

*"My child," he said in a voice soft and strong. "My poor child."*

*All she could do was look up at him in awe. A tear welled in one of his eyes and fell onto her forehead. In that instant, she knew where she had come from, what this place was, why she was here, and who the man was.*

*She thought too of the old man, and the dog, and the love they shared. As she thought of the dog, she heard a woof, and he was by her side, licking her face and wagging his stub of a tail. She leaned over and hugged the dog, thought for a moment, then, knowing what she would be giving up, she looked back at the man and said in a timid voice, "May we go back, please? He needs us."*

*The man nodded, as though he had known what she was going to ask.*

*"It was your time, child," he said sadly, "and the dog's time. Time is always something to wish there was more of.*

*"But there is a way you can be together again, if your desire, and your love, are so great."*

*She nodded her head. He bent forward and kissed the little girl on the forehead. The girl and the dog glowed brighter than the candles she had seen in the church. The two lights flowed together.*

The old man trudged through knee-deep snow in the morning sun, calling out the little girl's and the dog's names. Tears flowed down his cheeks.

He was halfway across the field between the railroad tracks and the back of the factory when he prayed out loud, "Please, God; please don't take them from me. In the name of Jesus Christ, your son, our lord, let them return to me. Please."

Church bells sounded in the distance. By his side resounded a chorus of familiar barks. Sinking to his knees, the old man wrapped his arms around the dog. The beast wiggled in his embrace and licked him in the face. In that moment, the old man realized that the little girl, though gone from him in body, was back with him nevertheless.

Standing, he reached down to the dog and said, "Come, my friends. Let us go home."

The townspeople never knew what happened to the little girl. From the old man's mutterings, they assumed she had wandered off to some other town. Memory of her soon faded.

The people in the town did notice that the old man's canine companion had taken on characteristics described variously as "amazing," "astounding," and even "miraculous." The dog seemed to understand the very words spoken not only by the old man but also by the people they met on the streets and those who continued to provide them with assorted food and other items. The dog's expressions, too, were those exhibited by people.

"I swear," one person commented; "if I didn't know better, I'd swear that dog is human."

The years passed. The old man and the dog lived far longer than anyone would have believed possible, and no one in the town was happier than those two, despite their humble lifestyle.

When, one day, the pair did not appear on their daily rounds begging, a handful of townspeople went to the switchman's shanty. There they found the companions. The old man was lying in his bed. The dog, now completely gray in the muzzle, lay at the old man's feet. As someone went to fetch the coroner, another remarked that he had never seen such serene, peaceful expressions.

The townspeople took up a collection and the two were buried side by side in the town cemetery. The following spring, no one could explain when three rosebushes grew from the soil, bushes whose branches gradually intertwined to form one massive bush that put forth the most radiant of white roses.

The town constable who had been on patrol the Christmas morning at the time of the little girl's disappearance had one other mystery he never mentioned to anyone. Around noon that day, he had been taking a shortcut back to the police station. He noticed a man's footprints in the snow in front of him. Halfway across the field between the railroad tracks and the back of the factory, the man's prints suddenly were joined by the tracks of a dog, as if the dog had dropped from out of the sky..

# Rainbow Horse

*(Two songs were the inspiration for this Christmas story — Canadian Gordon Lightfoot's ballad "Don Quixote," and American Mason Williams' instrumental, "Vancouver Island.")*

From a window in the tallest tower of his castle, the evil king looked out across the snow-covered fields and towns of the kingdom he had ruled through violence and fear for so many years.

His eyes narrowed as he thought of the final words gasped by the elderly seer to whose death bed he had been summoned only weeks before. The dying man had stared up at the ruler and wheezed, "Beware the rainbow horse on Christmas Day."

The king watched the falling snow and wondered still again how a rainbow could appear in the winter. The only multi-colored beams curving through the air he had ever seen had been in the sunshine following spring showers and summer thunderstorms. How, then, could a rainbow appear in the winter, and in what way did it tie in to a horse. Nevertheless, he had sent extra patrols throughout the countryside that morning and ordered his sergeants to ensure the castle's sentries were especially alert on this holiest of days.

High in the hills above the castle, an old man trudged through the snow from his hut to a lean-to that sheltered the only horse remaining from the small herd he had once possessed. Unlike the sleek and powerful horses that had pulled the wagons and carts he had once owned many years ago, this horse had never been anything but a plow horse. Nevertheless, the old man had always been the fondest of this steed for its friendly and gentle nature. He thought how the horse and he looked more alike every day, their bones protruding from frames no longer muscular and strong.

The horse nudged at him as he put on the saddle.

"Old friend," he whispered in the horse's ear, "I can no longer tolerate the weeping, frightened looks, and empty bellies of the people, especially the children. You and I no longer possess the strength we used to have but perhaps this holiest of days will somehow help us end the years of brutality that have brought so much anguish to our land."

Easing into the saddle and securing a sword rusty with years in his belt, the old man turned the horse into the snowy lane that led down from the mountains to the castle below. At the first house he passed, a woman emerged from the door and motioned to him to stop. Slowly making her way though the snow with the use of a twisted cane, the cloaked figure drew up to the horse.

"Here," she said; handing up to the man a pair of gloves. "These will keep your hands warm for the quest that lies ahead."

The man smiled his thanks and slipped on the gloves. "But how did you know …"

"I know," came the soft but firm reply from the wrinkled face looking up at him. "We all know. God speed."

The man and horse continued on. From beneath a towering juniper tree, a waif wrapped in a tattered cloak stepped out before them and thrust up a single flower.

The man smiled down at the girl and took the flower. Smelling its fragrance, he slipped it in the neck of his tunic.

Using sign language, he gestured down to the girl, "Thank you for the lovely flower, child. Where did you find such a bloom on a winter's day?" The girl's hands moved quickly in their reply, "The shepherd who watches over us all led me to this flower only an hour ago. It will bring you luck."

Flashing a shy smile, she turned, darted through the snow-covered bushes lining the narrow lane, and disappeared.

The man and horse continued on. The snow began falling more thickly. From a boulder a short distance from the road, a man surrounded by a herd of goats called out to the man, "Is that you, good neighbor? The unsteady breath of your steed and the soft clip clop he makes in the snow tell me you and your friend have started out on your journey."

The man slipped down from his rock and, using a cane to test the terrain ahead, made his way toward the lane. Reaching inside his cloak, he pulled out a scarf.

"Here, take this. It's an extra one. It will help keep you warm."

The old man reached down, took the scarf with one hand, and grasped the shepherd's hand with the other. "Old friend, you understand what I set out to do?"

"Of course," was the reply. "The news of a noble action flies ahead as if on the wings of a bird. Our thoughts go with you."

The old man gripped the shepherd's shoulder, than sat back up, wrapped the scarf around his neck, and smiled. "That is indeed more comfortable," he said. "Thank you." He took up the reins and continued on, as the shepherd turned and tap-tapped his way back to his herd.

A short way on, a small chapel sat at a crossroads. From beneath its shingled roof limped a young man holding a small bundle in his hand. The old man reined in the horse.

"This is for your horse, goodly father," the youth said. The old man reached down and discovered the bundle was a carefully embroidered sash.

"It belonged to my father many years gone," the youth said. "I believe perhaps your steed should wear it now as an emblem of the role he is about to play."

"And how come you to know what role my old friend is about to undertake?" questioned the old man as he carefully wrapped the sash around the horse's neck and tied the ends in a knot.

"The quest you have undertaken is for all of us," was the reply. "Now go, and know our prayers go with you."

The young man returned to the chapel, where he knelt and bowed his head. The old man watched him for a moment, then turned the horse away and continued down the mountain.

The town surrounding the castle was quiet, the streets empty, but as the horse walked past one alleyway, two children darted out at the old man. He reined in the horse and smiled down at them. Their clothes were patched and torn, and bare skin showed through. The girl nudged the boy, who reached in a pocket and pulled forth a twig loaded with berries.

"Well, my goodness; another fruitful offering," the old man murmured. He reached down and gathered the berries into his hand. "From whence came such fruit on a day such as this?"

"We were looking for something to eat at the back door of an inn and saw these berries lying in the snow," the girl replied. "And they were so pretty, we thought we would save them for you," the boy added.

"But how did you know …"

"Having a pretty thing to look at when you're cold makes you feel not so cold," the girl said. "When we hold one another to stay warm at night in the vestibule of the church, the cold is lessened when we look up at the beautiful stained glass windows."

The two children turned and raced back into the darkness of the alleyway. The old man watched them go, smiled sadly, and tucked the berries into the band of his hat.

A short distance on and he reached the main gate of the castle. Several sentries huddled around a fire. The old man hesitated. At that moment, a whirlwind of snow howled through the town and filled the air about the gate, creating a curtain of invisibility. The hold man encouraged the horse on. They passed, unseen, by the sentries, through the gatehouse, into the calm and silence of the castle courtyard.

The man looked up at a tower window from which a yellow light shone forth. He stared at the window and the evil king appeared, glaring down at the threadbare figure on horseback in the courtyard.

Pulling forth his sword and pointing it at the king, the old man cried, "In the name of the king who was born on this day, I tell you that your realm of evil has come to an end!"

The king stared down with wide eyes, then bellowed to his soldiers. The sentries rushed through the gatehouse into the courtyard while soldiers poured out of the barracks. The old man reared the horse in the air, circling and wheeling and swinging his sword as the soldiers closed on him with swords and spears.

For a time, the only sounds were of metal ringing on metal, the shouts of the combatants, and the screaming of the old horse.

A sudden boom crashed down from above. The soldiers held back on their attack and looked up, as did the king from his balcony. A hole had appeared in the snow clouds above. A beam from the now revealed sun shone down on the old man and his horse. The soldiers shrank back and the wicked king, seeing warrior and steed illuminated in the sudden light, could only stare and tremble.

For, glowing like newborn snow, was the man's long white beard. The rich brown coat of the horse shimmered. The red gloves the man wore were the reddest red the king had ever seen, and the yellow flower in the neck of the man's tunic was brighter than a summer's field of sunflowers. The blue sash around the horse's neck was as rich an azure as the deepest ocean. As brilliant a green as emeralds was the scarf wrapped around the old man's neck. And crowning it all, in the band of the old man's hat, was a cluster of berries impossibly powerfully orange.

Here was the rainbow horse that had been prophesized. Not from a rainbow in the sky; rather, a rainbow of humble items, gathered and presented to the old man through love, to help him on a journey in which he was willing to sacrifice his life for that which is decent and honorable.

The king's anger and hatred were so great, despite his fear, he shouted at his soldiers to continue their attack. This they did, stabbing at the old man as he returned blow for blow, and thrusting at the old horse as it wheeled and charged about them.

Suddenly, with a great roar, townspeople and people who had hurried down from the countryside flooded through the gatehouse into the castle courtyard. With axes and pitchforks, shovels and brooms, rakes and clubs, they flew to the aid of the old man. A stone hurled from the crowd struck the evil king in the head. Staggering forward, he toppled over the balcony railing and fell to his death. Seeing their leader thus fallen, the soldiers still standing threw down their weapons and begged for mercy.

Lying in the middle of the carnage lay the old man, one hand resting on the neck of his prone horse. Both bled profusely. Slowly the man's hand slipped down, the old horse's flanks stopped heaving, and a final breath came from them both.

With the death of the evil king, his remaining soldiers pledged their allegiance to a council of good and wise leaders chosen by people throughout the kingdom. And the land prospered, and all were happy and content.

As for the old man and his horse, they were buried where they had fallen in the courtyard, and a monument of granite and marble was erected above them.

Every spring and summer when showers rejuvenate the land, as each rain comes to an end, the people look upward. They watch as the sun shines forth, and a multi-hued rainbow arcs brilliantly across the land. And in the sunny mist in that immense curve of multiple colors, the people can see the old man and his horse flying across the sky, vibrant and watchful once again and forever after.

# El Burrito de la Navidad

*(The inspiration for this Christmas story was composer Mason Williams' instrumental "Flamenco Lingo.")*

❄   ❄   ❄

To this day, the villagers of Santa Maria, nestled high on the eastern slopes of the Sierra Madres, do not know from where came the burro. All they know is that little Carlitos Martinez was the one who found the animal, on the eve of la Navidad when the winter winds swept in cold and bitter from El Golf de Mexico.

Ricardo Villa and Pedro Gomez insisted it was they who caused the small, gray donkey to come to Santa Maria. After all, they pointed out, if they had not led their flock of sheep past the grove of pinon trees where Carlitos was tending to the injured animal, and so added their expertise to his ineffective efforts, the animal surely would have died.

This claim was disputed by the Reyes brothers. It was they, the three men said, who came upon the shepherds and Carlitos along the road to Santa Maria. They were returning from the provincial capital of Hidalgo, where they had driven their World War I surplus flatbed truck to bring back a shipment of wares for their store in Santa Maria. Making room amongst the boxes, sacks and barrels for the burro and the muchacho, they pointed out, allowed a far faster return to Santa Maria than if the two had stayed with Ricardo's and Pedro's flock.

This was an argument that carried on for many weeks in the local cantina, and was one of the causes of the occasional fights that took place in that adobe building's smoky interior. Such was the way of Santa Maria – arguments and altercations. Forgotten in this particular argument was the fact that it was, after all, Carlitos who first found the burro.

Adjacent to the building that served as both home and carpenter shop for Carlitos and his father was a small shed for their milk cow and chickens. It was here that the Reyes brothers helped Carlitos make the burro comfortable on a bed of hay in an empty stall.

When Carlitos told his father about the animal, Esteban Martinez was not happy. One more mouth to feed, he told his son; an animal that was not useful, as were the cow and chickens. It was the money from their milk and eggs, he pointed out to the boy, that supplemented the meager living he earned in his carpenter shop. Of what use was this small, injured burro?

Carlitos had known his father would not want to keep the burro. It wasn't that Senor Martinez did not love his son. He did, but seldom showed it. Carlitos often thought his father's behavior was linked to the fact that the death date carved on his mother's gravestone was the day he had been born.

The elder Martinez, after much grumbling, told the boy that he could keep the burro but only if he found some way that the animal could earn its way, helping with the Martinez casa income as did the family cow and chickens.

Carlitos named his burro "Estrella." It was by the unusually bright light of stars on that night in late Diciembre that had led him to the little animal, so it seemed appropriate to name his new friend after those stars.

Carlitos and Estrella became a common site on the narrow, dirt streets of Santa Maria in the days of the New Year. The burro, recovered from its injuries, followed the boy like a faithful dog. Mindful of his father's daily admonishments that the burro must earn its keep, Carlitos began gathering twigs and sticks in the forests on the outskirts of Santa Maria, tying them into bundles onto Estrella's small but sturdy back, and selling the wood as kindling to the housewives of the village.

At the end of each day, Carlitos gave a handful of pesos to his father. Esteban Martinez grumbled about the small amount of money as he placed the coins in the pocket of his carpenter's apron.

Estrella was a docile and eager animal. Carlitos soon devised a sling for the burro's back by which he was able to carry woven baskets of chicken eggs and clay jars of their cow's milk. Before, customers had come to the carpenter shop for these items. Now, with the help of Estrella, Carlitos was able to deliver to the casas of the villagers. The pesos increased each day, and Senor Martinez gave his son a begrudging smile at the end of the day when he placed the money in his carpenter's apron.

The days grew longer in Santa Maria. The wind blowing in from El Golf de Mexico that growled through the streets of the village in winter now became a balmy breeze that caressed the sun-drenched adobe buildings. The fields around the village burst into their spring tapestry of purple, yellow, white and lavender.

One day, Padre Roberto was strolling through these fields. The old friar was the only one remaining of the four Franciscan brothers who had once been assigned to the mission. Those were the days when Santa Maria was a growing and bustling town instead of the sleepy, fading village it had become.

He came upon a group of children gathering flowers. In the middle of this group of laughing and shouting children were Carlitos and Estrella. On the little gray burro's back were several children. Walking alongside was a watchful Carlitos. Even Estrella seemed to be smiling.

It was a scene to warm Padre Roberto's heart. It had been years since he had observed such laughter and gaiety in the village.

Later in the day, the children brought bouquets of flowers to the mission to decorate the window sills, niches and altar. The dark interior of the mission took on a look of joy.

As spring turned into summer, Carlitos and his little burro worked harder than ever. In addition to gathering and selling twigs and sticks for kindling, and delivering milk and eggs, Estrella was a welcome site to the workers toiling in the fields under the blazing sun.

The donkey and his companion brought cool water to quench their fierce thirsts, and when the sun was at its highest and they took their much deserved siesta breaks, here came the burro and the muchacho with their midday meals. Always, Estrella seemed to have a smile on his face, a fact that led to much laughter and gentle teasing.

Carlitos continued to give his day's earnings to his father every evening. Esteban Martinez smiled more now, and occasionally reached down and hugged his son. On evenings when the day's carpentry was completed, he helped the boy put down Estrella for the night in the shed he shared with the cow and chickens.

The change in season passed over a village that knew much better prosperity and harmony than it had known in years. Even Juanita Diaz and Eva Morales -- two neighboring housewives who had carried on a years-long feud for reasons long forgotten -- were speaking to one another again. Feuds and fussing had long been the way of Santa Maria but now such bickering seemed a thing of the past.

The autumn sun glowed down warmly on the mountain village as a bountiful harvest was gathered by happy townspeople. Grumbling and arguing in the cantina were replaced by songs and laughter. The clicking of dominos and checkers became commonplace on the town square again, as the old men felt the sun easing their ancient bones while they cackled and teased one other.

Padre Roberto was delighted when the number of people gathering at the old mission on Sunday mornings steadily grew. Carlitos had always attended Mass faithfully. Estrella now accompanied him to the door, and waited outside along with the other animals – burros, horses, dogs and even a few cats – that had come to the mission with their owners.

One Sunday toward harvest's end, the good padre was surprised to see Esteban Martinez walk into the mission with his son and take a seat. It was the first time in many a year that the carpenter had come to church. Every Sunday after that, father and son attended Mass together. The old Franciscan friar's heart glowed with the autumn sun.

And now the first winds of early winter began to whisper through the mountain village. This year, though, the people of Santa Maria were better prepared for the upcoming months of cold and barren weather. The granaries were near overflowing, the pantries were filled with preserved fruits and vegetables, and the haylofts and storerooms had food in abundance for people and beasts alike to see them through the months ahead.

Padre Roberto was fully aware of this renewed feeling of contentment in the village. One evening, he suggested to members of the church board that it was time for Santa Maria to once again have organized activities honoring la Navidad.

This idea was taken up with much enthusiasm by the board, which quickly began organizing the events. One highlight would be a parade through the town, and leading the parade, it was agreed, would be the town's children and their animals.

And so it came to pass. On the day of la Navidad, a parade of children and animals, decorated wagons and carts, and musicians with their guitars, trumpets and drums flowed through Santa Maria's narrow, winding streets.

And at the head of the parade, among the children and animals, were Carlitos and Estrella. That they should lead the way somehow seemed natural to everyone. Estrella had ribbons of green, red and white festooning his bridle.

Among the laughter, shouting, music and singing, only old Anna Juarez noticed that the burro seemed to have a sad look in his eyes, a look remarkably different from the good humor that usually illuminated from the burro's face.

The parade culminated on the town square with mariachi bands, games and prizes, several piñatas, and the singing of carols. These festivities were followed by a more dignified procession to the mission, where Padre Roberto performed a Mass for la Navidad, complete with the traditional carols of old sung by the newly organized town choir, and joined in by a very enthusiastic congregation. At the front of the old mission was a Nativity scene with Mary, Joseph and the Christ Child. Esteban Martinez had carved the figures in his carpenter shop and presented them to a delighted Padre Roberto only a week before.

Later that evening, Carlitos and his father led Estrella into the warmth of the shed, and ensured the burro and other animals were snug for the night. Carlitos' head was nodding after the long, busy day and evening, and the carpenter carried his son back to the house and hence to his bed.

Sometime during that night, Carlitos awakened with a start. He knew not why, but sensed that something was wrong. Wrapping a serape around himself, he lighted a lantern and hurried out to the shed. The chickens were roosting quietly on their perches and the cow was lying in its stall, chewing its cud. But Estrella's stall was empty. The burro was gone.

The muchacho ran back outside. All was quiet in the crisp night air. Running to the top of a rise behind the house, he looked out over the still fields bathed in moonlight. A short distance ahead was Estrella, trotting briskly away from Santa Maria.

"Estrella!" the boy shouted, and ran toward the burro. The animal stopped and turned as Carlitos dashed up to its side.

Carlitos hugged the burro around the neck, illuminated by starlight that shown down with fierce brightness from the heavens.

The boy looked into the little animal's eyes and what shown forth from them joined the light from above to help him understand the burro; why it had come to Santa Maria a year before, and why it was time to leave.

Tears of sadness mixed with tears of joy as he hugged Estrella, who neighed softly and nuzzled him in return.

"Adios, mi amigo," he said softly. "Muchas gracias, y vaya con Dios."

The burro nuzzled him one last time, then turned and set out again on the never-ending mission to bring peace on Earth, goodwill toward men.

In the days to come, the villagers of Santa Maria were baffled and saddened by the disappearance of the little burro. Esteban Martinez consoled his son and was surprised at how well the boy took the loss.

The carpenter used some of the dinero his son and burro had earned in the past year to buy another burro, a little brown animal that Carlitos named Jubilo, since joy was what had come again to the Martinez casa, and to the entire village.

The widow Anna Juarez told anyone in the marketplace who would listen to her that Estrella had left Santa Maria because he had done what he had come to do. She was just an old woman, though, and touched in the head, and everyone ignored her.

Santa Maria did not forget Estrella, but as the months wore on and turned into years, and harmony and contentment filled the village, and the winds from El Gulf de Mexico danced through the mountains and the sun shown down its warmth, the people of Santa Maria were busy with the toil and laughter and work and songs of daily life and the turn of the seasons.

The village was a happy place, and Carlitos and his father and Jubilo – they too were happy.

# Jubal Kinkaid's Christmas Odyssey

*(The inspiration for this Christmas story was composer Mason Williams' instrumental "Vancouver Island.")*

The rising sun cast a golden glow as Jubal Kinkaid strode across the yard toward the stable, his battered cavalry boots crunching in the snow that had fallen overnight.

He glanced back at the cabin. A wisp of smoke from the chimney indicated that the fire he had started a few minutes earlier had taken hold. He had dressed quietly so as not to awaken Jessie. Whenever his wife did wake up and he didn't respond to her call, the six acorns he had left in the bowl on the bedside table for her searching fingers would tell her that he had gone on an errand that would take him off their farm for several hours.

An assortment of clucking, mooing, baaing, grunting and neighing greeted him from the stable's warm, earthy interior as he pulled open one of its double doors. He worked quickly to saddle Nicodemus, the chestnut Arabian pushing playfully against him. Jubal tightened the cinches, his fingers pausing for a moment as they always did, on the fading CSA inscription embossed by the saddle horn.

He led Nicodemus into the crisp December air, shut the stable door, and swung in an easy motion into the saddle.

"Husband, where are you going?"

Jessie was leaning against one of the porch posts, her favorite shawl wrapped about her. Her head was turned and tilted slightly as she strove to catch any sounds that would reveal what lay before her.

Jubal frowned. He had hoped to be gone and on his way home before the only woman he had ever loved had awakened.

"Jessie, you go on back to bed now. I started a fire. I'm just … going for a ride; working out the kinks in Nicodemus and me."

"Oh, Jubal!" Jessie shook her head slowly. "I know where you're going. You're going up to the old homestead, aren't you? And on this, of all mornings in the year. You just won't let the past sleep, will you? Darling, you can't change what happened. All that's left up there are burnt timbers and broken bricks."

"And Jack and Annie," Jubal interrupted. "They're up there too, don't forget."

"No, husband; only their graves. Our children are in heaven. They've been with the Lord ever since that day."

Jubal shuddered, as he always did when he heard words that reminded him of that day – of pounding hoof beats, shouted orders, flaming torches, screams from inside the house, and gunshots that left two small figures in nightshirts lying among the green shoots of late spring. And he hadn't been there for them. He had been a hundred miles away, with General Forrest crushing a much larger Yankee force at Brice's Crossroads. He hadn't been there to protect his son and daughter from the Yankees' murderous musket balls, or his wife from the flames that had seared and scarred her face.

He kneed Nicodemus up to the porch steps and leaned down to touch the face that had always been, and would always be, beautiful to him.

"I just need to go, Jessie; just a short visit. It does me good. I won't stay long. I'll be back in time to help you pluck that tom turkey hanging on the back porch."

His wife reached up to caress his hand.

"Go on then, Jubal. But go with a heart of love and forgiveness, not one of hatred and bitterness. Please. For you and for me, and for our Lord."

"All right Jessie," the horseman replied as he leaned back into his saddle and reined Nicodemus toward the road. "I'll be back soon."

But as he trotted down the lane, his thoughts smoldered like burning embers aimed at the souls of the raiders who had ripped his children from him.

He urged Nicodemus into a gallop and the big horse's muscles rippled and flexed, his hooves sending snow flying as he raced past the snow-covered woods and fields. Startled birds burst from cover with a flurry of wings as horse and rider dashed along the lane. They splashed icily across the babbling waters of a ford, and a white dove darted close by them.

After some minutes and miles, Jubal slowed Nicodemus to a trot. The horse pulled on the reins, still eager to relive those yesterdays in western Tennessee when he and his rider had been at the vanguard of raids that had wreaked havoc behind Union lines.

The early winter sun was at the treetops when Jubal turned his horse onto the log and plank bridge leading to the hilltop that was his destination. Nicodemus' hooves sounded out a hollow drumming as they pranced on the wide wooden planks. Jubal's head jerked as a white dove shot by in front of them.

Near the hill's crown, he swung out of the saddle and led his horse to the pair of stone markers rising like silent ghosts from the ground's blanket of snow. With bowed head, he stood silent and motionless, but his head swirled with images of what had happened, and the painful reminder that Jack and Jennie were gone because of the human weaknesses of violence, hatred and delusions.

Nicodemus' sudden neighing caused his owner's head to jerk around. Leading a horse toward them was a man wearing a faded blue coat and slouch hat. Jubal stared toward this apparition. A Yankee! Instinctively, he whipped out his old Colt revolver, aimed at the stranger, and fired.

His aim was true. So too was the timing of a white dove that flashed down between the two men. Pistol ball and bird collided in a white and red burst of feathers and blood. The stranger dropped to his knees and held out his hands toward Jubal.

"Friend, for God's sake; don't shoot! I'm unarmed. I mean you no harm."

Jubal let his hand drop to his side but he still gripped the pistol.

"You're a damn Yankee!" he snarled. A further realization hit him.

"You're one of them!" he shouted. "You're one of the filthy raiders that murdered my son and daughter and left my wife sightless. Why else would you be here?"

Tears ran down the stranger's face and dripped from his gray beard into the pristine snow.

"Reb, forgive me. There hasn't been a day since that day I haven't thought about what we did. Such horror; such a crime! But I didn't know your little ones would be gunned down; I swear I didn't. I would have stopped it if I'd of known, or at least tried. Was bad enough we'd been burning the homes of innocent folks, but this was the first time children had been killed. Oh, God; forgive me!" He bowed his head and his shoulders shook.

Jubal felt a warm glow on his face. The sun was now shining down from just above the tree line. Its warmth flowed down into his chest and he felt a strange, peaceful sensation. He holstered his pistol and walked up to the stranger.

"On your feet, stranger," he said in a choked voice. "I'm sorry too; I was wrong to fire on you. My wife was right; what's done is done. The war's over. We all need to move on."

He helped the man to his feet. The two men looked down silently on the two gravestones.

"Jack and Annie," the stranger said surprisingly. "Those are a lot like my children's names – Zack and Fannie."

Jubal looked at his former adversary. "Well, I'll be darned. Are they in good health? Are they happy?"

The stranger gave a sad smile. "Yes, their mother and I love them deeply. And we have another one on the way. If it's a boy … what's your name, friend?"

"Jubal."

"Well, by golly, if it's a boy, we'll name him Jubal."

"And if it's a girl, do you think you could call her Jessie? That's my wife's name."

The stranger's smile widened. "Why, of course; it would be an honor."

The two men – the old Confederate cavalryman and the old Union cavalryman – looked at one another for a moment. One held out his hand and the other took it.

"Merry Christmas, Reb."

"Merry Christmas, Yank."

They mounted their steeds and pulled away on the journeys back to their respective homes. Toward the hill's base, Jubal turned and looked back toward the hilltop, where the two markers and piles of burnt timbers now lay not just in silence but also in peace.

He urged Nicodemus into a gallop and gave out a long and loud rebel yell. From across the white-covered landscape, a Yankee whoop echoed a reply.

The big horse covered the miles back home in what seemed to Jubal to be only a fraction of the time the journey out had taken. As the cold air stung his cheeks, he mused that maybe his now-lightened heart had something to do with his pace.

Nicodemus turned off the lane and up the path toward the waiting buildings. They had only just slowed before the stable when Jessie darted out the front door of the house, dashed down the steps, and ran across the snow toward her husband.'

"Jubal! Jubal! I can see! I can see! Oh, sweet God in heaven! My dearest husband! I can see!" Jessie's face glowed as bright as the Christmas Day sun now streaming down from a crisp blue sky.

Jubal slid out of the saddle and his wife rushed into his waiting arms. They hugged and then kissed, and he looked down into his wife's face. Her clear eyes looked back up at him.

"Jessie, darling! What happened! … How? … When?" he choked.

"Oh, Jubal" she cried. "I was by the fireplace, about an hour ago, plucking the turkey for our Christmas dinner when a loud popping sound came from the flames in the hearth. It sounded almost like a gunshot, so loud and sharp. And just like that, I could see for the first time since … since that day. It's a miracle, Jubal! It's a miracle for this, the day we celebrate the birth of our Savior!"

Husband and wife hugged tightly again and Jubal's thoughts for a moment went back to the clearing on the hilltop, just an hour before, when the pistol ball meant for his enemy had never reached its target.

Still hugging one another, Jubal and Jessie led Nicodemus into the stable. There, for the first time in years, she helped him unsaddle the faithful horse, rub him down, turn him into his stall, and give him fresh water and an armful of hay.

Their arms around one another, they walked back across the yard, up the porch steps and into the cabin, where a renewed life awaited.

Back outside, the snow began to fall again, its quiet shushing sound like the peal of tiny bells ringing out their eternal song of hope and love. Through the falling flakes, a white dove circled over the quiet homestead -- a Prince of Peace blessing the scene below.

# Valentine's Day

♥ ♥ ♥

# More Precious than Gold

As he emptied grain sacks into the feed barrel, the man's thoughts wandered forward to Valentine's Day and how he hadn't decided yet what to give his wife.

"Don't be concerned," said a quiet voice. A figure with a long white beard, wearing tunic and sandals, stood in the sunlight filtering through the barn door.

Startled, the man asked, "Who are you?"

"Saint Valentine," the stranger replied. "Hundreds of years ago in another land, an emperor unjustly imprisoned me. The letters of hope I was able to smuggle out to my friends were the basis for greetings of love now exchanged every February 14."

The man fastened the barrel's lid. "But I am concerned," he said. "Valentine's Day is les than a week away. I love my wife and want to give her something special. I just don't know what."

The stranger walked toward him. "Here," he said, "take hold of my sleeve."

The man hesitated, then reached out. The cloth felt cool to his touch. He had a sensation of being weightless; then he found himself looking down across the countryside. Fields and woods were a patchwork of brown, gray and green. Roads were thin, straight lines connecting towns and farms. The late winter wind whirled around the two as the stranger pointed and said, "Observe."

The man looked down on a small back yard. An old man was pushing two children in a tire swing as the three laughed and shouted. "They're his grandchildren," the stranger said. "They visit him several times a month."

Next door, a boy carrying a basketball gave his mother a quick hug as he ran through the living room and out the front door.

Several miles from town, in a secluded farmhouse, the man saw a woman with graying hair writing at her dining room table. "She's sending a letter to her father. He lives in a nursing home in another state," the stranger said.

Now they were looking down on a bedroom in a duplex, and they watched as a young boy was tucked into bed by his sister, not much older than he was. She began reading to him from a storybook. When he had fallen asleep, she put aside the book, turned out the bedside lamp, and left the door open a few inches as she went out, so that a thin beam of light from the other room shone across her brother's bed.

Other sights flew by far below: a father reaching out and tousling his son's hair as the two sat in a rodeo bleachers … a church supper where a woman was bringing a plate of food to her elderly aunt … a boy in a pickup truck dozing outside a grocery store, waiting to give his kid sister a ride home from her after-school job … a woman hugging her husband as he stood at the basin shaving … a girl sitting on the floor with her phone, consoling a friend who had just broken up with her boyfriend … a mobile home in which a mother packed her children's lunch boxes, carefully placing a dessert bar between the apple and peanut butter and jelly sandwich … a man leaving a funny cartoon on his wife's sewing machine ….

Other visions flashed before them, and then they were back in the barn. The angle of the sunlight shining on the boards opposite the door hadn't changed. The man looked confused.

"The cards you share on Valentine's Day," the stranger explained; "the greetings you exchange – these are symbols of something greater. They represent the love you give all year long, not just on one day. The little things you do, the everyday gestures, the simplest gifts …"

The stranger reached down, scooped up some dirt and held it out toward the man.

"If you gave a handful of dirt to one who is special to you, but you gave it with all the love in your heart and it was the finest gift you could think to offer, then that gift would be more precious than a chest of gold."

The man thought, then smiled and nodded his head. The stranger turned and stepped through the barn door. Just before he disappeared around the corner, he looked back over his shoulder. At the same moment, the stranger and the man called out together, "Happy Valentine's Day!"

# The Missing Piece of Valentine Candy

The driver of the big rig and the hitchhiker had been traveling westward for three hours along a snow-swept I-40. Their conversation had spanned a variety of topics as the truck rumbled down the dark highway, but just west of Nashville, the talk died away. The only sounds were the muffled roar of the engine, the hum of the cab heater, and the slapping of the windshield wipers. An occasional buzzing voice from the CB told of another car in the ditch or jack-knifed truck.

The hitchhiker glanced down at the heart-shaped candy box resting on the seat between them. "That for someone special?"

The driver chuckled. "You bet. Someone real special." He was silent for a moment. Then, feeling the familiarity and trust that often come to strangers thrown together on the same path, he looked over at the hitchhiker. "You ever been in love so much you thought you'd bust with how good it felt? Real true love?"

"I'm not sure," the hitchhiker replied. "You?"

The driver nodded his head. "Oh, yeah. I'll tell you, though. It snuck up and blindsided me before I knew what was happening."

The hitchhiker wiggled into a more comfortable position. "So, how'd it happen?"

"I'd been driving for the same company for more than 30 years when they cut way back on my loads, and I had to start looking for another part-time job. Didn't have any luck, though. When you're over 60, they figure they'll hire the younger fellas instead. Then my sister told me a farm out toward the county line needed an extra hand, so I hustled out there one afternoon.

"Woman who owned the place, her husband had died a few years back – cancer, I think it was – and she was runnin' the place by herself. Several dozen head of cattle, a little cotton, some chickens, a truck garden. He'd left her well enough off, but she needed someone to kind of ease her load a bit.

"We worked out a deal, and she fixed me up in a real nice little guest house out back by the barn. She'd decorated it herself, and I felt like I was staying in some big celebrity suite at a fancy hotel. Matter of fact, there wasn't nothin' Bertha couldn't do, it seemed. She handled a tractor and a combine like a pro, doctored the cattle as well as any vet, canned a slew of vegetables, and sold extra eggs in town.

"As busy as she was there on the farm, she was just as active out in the community. She was in her church choir, was a member of the women's group, and was on various committees for carnivals and revivals and such. Tuesday evenings, she had a group of women over to play bridge. She was a member of the county election commission, and did some volunteer work with the senior care center. Oh, and a couple of times a week, she went to an aerobics class at the high school. She had kind of an ongoing weight problem.

"Well, the months went by, and I was really enjoying myself – maybe a fourth of my time on the road; the rest of the time on the farm. And Bertha was a joy to be around – always smiling and encouraging, and never losing her patience with a stubborn cow or a dog in her garden or whatever.

"You know how when you really care for someone, you're happy that they're happy? I felt that way about Bertha. But I realized that I also felt something else for her. I had fallen in love with her. I didn't let on, though. We'd gotten to be friends but, after all, I was just the hired hand, right?"

"Then one night just about a year ago, we were sitting in the living room with our coffee. She had made some comment about trying to figure out how to juggle several meetings that weekend, and I had said something about her having a real full life. She looked at me kind of funny when I told her that, and I said, 'Well, shoot Bertha. What else do you want?'

"She set down her coffee cup and put both hands in her lap and looked down. Then she looked back up at me and a tear ran from each eye and she said, 'All I want is someone to love me.' All I could do was stare at her, and she jumped up and ran down the hall, and I heard her bedroom door slam shut."

The hitchhiker heard the hesitation in the driver's voice, and glanced over. The glow from the dashboard lights illuminated the tear running down his cheek. The driver rubbed his hand across his face, swallowed, and continued.

"At first, all I could do was sit there. Then it hit me. All those meetings and smiles and chores and singing and everything were like a box of candy with the best piece missing. Bertha didn't have that one thing we all need. She had a ton of love to give, but that wasn't enough. She needed someone to love her back, to really love her. Well, she had that someone – me.

"I jumped up from my chair and ran down the hall but her door was locked. I put my shoulder to it and practically ripped it from the hinges. Bertha was sitting on the floor against the wall, just sitting there with her legs in front of her and her arms dangling down, like a rag doll. She looked up at me and said it again, in a voice so soft and sad – 'All I want is someone to love me.'

"I knelt down next to her and took her in my arms and said, 'Bertha, I love you.' And she said, 'Oh, Joe; I love you too.' She hugged me back, and that's when I felt I was gonna bust, I felt so full and good on the inside."

The driver reached into a jacket pocket, pulled out a handkerchief, and blew his nose. Neither man spoke for several minutes. The driver looked over at the hitchhiker, who was smiling down at the heart-shaped box of valentine candy.

"Look here, friend. My exit is just ahead. I can either let you out there at the truck-stop and you can grab another ride, or you can come on home and spend the night with my wife and me. We'll put you up in the guest house since it's empty now. Bertha always enjoys company, and she fixes a whale of a meal."

The traveler grinned. "You talked me into it. I'd like that. I'd like to meet the special lady this box of candy is for."

The driver nodded his head as he down-shifted onto the exit ramp. "She's special, all right. She's the most wonderful woman in the world."

That was good enough for the shy young man. They talked a bit longer, and then he took his leave. When Willie's mule-drawn wagon passed Dummy a mile up the road, Dummy was humming quietly to himself, kicking at small rocks and reaching down every so often to put a more colorful one in his pocket.

When Willie returned from the Pacific two years later, he and Flavia were married. She instructed friends helping with invitations to be sure Dummy received one. However, not realizing the strong bond between the two, they failed to send him an invitation.

The afternoon of the ceremony, Dummy stood behind some trees across the road from the hewn-log country church and listened to the music that came from within. He watched as the wedding party emerged and headed toward the tables of food in the grove adjacent to the church. His joy at seeing his dear friend so radiant and obviously happy overcame the loneliness and misery he had been feeling.

During Willie's and her courtship, Flavia had explained to her fiancée the simple goodness within Dummy, and a bond had developed between the two men. Dummy smiled as he watched Willie and Flavia, and all the guests, laughing and talking as they thronged about the waiting food. He raised his hands palms outward toward the newlyweds in a gesture he faintly understood to be some sort of blessing, then turned and shuffled home. He stopped occasionally to pick up a rock to slip into his pocket.

Dummy was a frequent visitor to Willie's and Flavia's home. He didn't say much but he enjoyed helping Flavia wash clothes and tend to the chickens, and helping Willie chop wood and work in the garden.

He was there the evening Willie was out of town helping folks register to vote, the evening when a rougher group of men got liquored up and decided to pay Flavia a call. Dummy had left for his shack shortly after sharing supper with Flavia but had instinctively sat down in the shadows where the drive turned onto the road. He was still waiting when the men approached.

The group had several lanterns with them. Their glow showed Dummy scrambling to his feet, holding a club fashioned from a tree branch. The men halted, surprised to see him. Dummy stood there holding his club.

What they saw on his face would have been enough to make them leave but one troublemaker skulking at the back of the group egged them on.

Up in the house, Flavia heard the commotion. She grabbed a lantern and Willie's .45 pistol that he'd brought back from the war, and ran down the drive. As she got close enough to see what was happening, she fired twice into the ground, and the gang skedaddled, leaving Dummy on one knee. Flavia fired off a couple more rounds to be sure the men had gone, and then helped Dummy to his feet. He was still holding his club.

When Willie returned home early the next morning, he found Dummy on a cot on the porch with bandages on his face and around his ribs. Flavia explained what had happened, and Willie's face tightened. He gently readjusted the bandages, then went to shantytown to make some inquiries. He tracked down and talked to a half dozen men with bruises, cracked bones and hangovers, and made sure they realized his wife and his friend were not to be bothered again.

Eight months later, Dummy was pacing on the front porch when Willie carried out the squalling baby the midwife had delivered. He let his friend hold the infant, and Dummy's grin was as big as the grin on his face the day he had watched Flavia and Willie emerge from the church.

Dummy had three friends now. Two years later he had a fourth friend when a little sister joined Willie Junior. Octavia was born in a hospital, and Dummy was waiting on the porch with little Willie when Willie and Flavia brought home the new baby. For the second time in his life, Dummy felt the pleasure of holding a newborn baby.

The years passed, years filled with good times and hard, laughter and tears. The toughest time for Dummy was on a simmering day in August 1967 when he stood with the rest of the family while an Army honor guard fired a volley and the casket of Private First Class Willie Carver Jr. was lowered into the ground in the cemetery next to the church where Flavia and Willie Sr. had been married. Dummy wondered if he might have been able to help little Willie stay alive if he had been with him at that place the others called Quang Tri.

More years passed; years filled with sunshine and rain showers, hard work and play. On a summer's night in 1979, Dummy stood on the porch with Willie and Flavia when Octavia and Darnell brought home little

Arturo. The infant was Willie's and Flavia's first grandchild and, by bond of love and friendship, also a first grandchild for Dummy. The parents let Dummy hold the baby, and the child and the man with an intellect of a child smiled at each other.

It became a family tradition that Dummy would be waiting on the porch and would briefly hold the growing family's newborn infants when they came home from the hospital. In the two decades that followed, Dummy welcomed nine more babies this way, and gave each one his own, simple blessing.

Two weeks ago, Dummy was there to receive the first in a new generation. He's 75 years old now and shuffles even more when he walks, and trembles when he sits. But he held Flavia's and Willie's great granddaughter with the same gentle care he has held all the other children.

After the rest of the family had gone in the house, Dummy stayed outside on the porch glider with one of the younger children. It was a warm Midsouth evening and through an open window, Flavia heard the child question the old man.

"Gran'paw Dummy, why you be so nice to us?"

Flavia paused to hear Dummy's reply, and she reached out with both hands to grip the table when he said in slow halting words, "Your gran'maw, she done give me a turtle."

The same silver moonlight that shone down onto the old man and the little boy sitting on the porch, the same moonlight that shone through the window onto the grey-haired woman standing by the table, also shone down across the countryside, along the waters of the Loosahatchie River, up a meandering creek, across the bottom lands, onto a small clearing in which a tiny mound of dirt was circled with a neat ring of small colorful rocks picked from the roadsides; a mound still carefully tended seven decades later with the love of one friend for another.

# Loosahatchie Love Across The Pacific

*(The following story is based on fading memories of shipmates, ports of call and life at sea. The tale itself, though, is fiction. Then again, as long as the love between a man and a woman is one of the most powerful forces in the world, maybe what is described here will happen someday ... or perhaps it already has.)*

*"I have my ship, and all her flags are a'flyin'.*
*She is all that I have left, and music is her name."*
*(from Crosby, Stills and Nash's "Southern Cross")*

The first time I saw Troob Kincaid was in San Diego harbor. I was standing the quarterdeck's 1200-1600 watch. The USS Wolf and other ships in Cruiser/Destroyer Group Five around us was fairly quiet in the midday heat as Kincaid staggered up the brow to the quarterdeck. His left shoulder sagged under the weight of his duffel bag, and his right shoulder drooped down from the weight of a guitar case and banjo case.

He set down the two cases, pivoted to the stern and saluted, and said, "Permission to come aboard?" He pulled his orders from the breast pocket of his dress blues and handed them to me. I told the messenger of the watch to take this newest crewmember down to the ship's office. Just before they disappeared through the hatch to the oh-two level, I asked, "Where you from, Kincaid?"

He grinned and said, "A green little piece of heaven in Tennessee, on the banks of the Loosahatchie River. I'll sing it some for you once I get settled."

I didn't know what he meant by that last comment but by the time we got underway a few weeks later for an 11-month West Pacific cruise, the rest of the crew and I had come to appreciate the musical talents of Troob Kincaid. He could play that guitar and that banjo like nobody's business and he had a pretty fair singing voice to go along with his strumming and picking.

I recall coming back from liberty late one Saturday night. The sound of a guitar drifted across the pier. Kincaid was up in the bow sitting on a capstan. Several members of Deck Division were seated around him listening as he sang about front porch evenings and hound dogs sprawled out and old folks in rocking chairs. The song Kincaid was singing sort of tied together the way a sailor is torn between heading out to sea and returning to the folks at home.

The morning we hauled in our mooring lines and shoved out into the harbor to the farewells of family members and friends gathered on the pier, Kincaid slipped away from the special sea and anchor detail to bring out his banjo and race through a lively little number he later told me was called "Travelin' Music." It was the sort of song you had to smile and tap your foot to. Several of the men in my division told me it helped make the parting a bit easier for the wives and girlfriends and kids left standing on the pier, watching us leave on a cruise that would last almost a year.

Among all the exercises, task forces, ports of call, excitement and monotony of that particular Westpac, the one thing that stands out is Kincaid and his music. It was sort of like the gravy the cooks ladled over our steaks down on the mess decks. We could have done without it, but having it on there made things a whole lot more tasty and lively.

When we stopped off in Pearl Harbor to replenish and go through all those briefings, it gave the crew the opportunity for several days of liberty in Hawaii. Some of the machinist's mates and boiler techs from M and B divisions told how they were driving a rental car along Hwy. 750 up in the Waianae Mountains when they passed through Kunia. There was Kincaid sitting on a picnic table in a roadside park picking away on his banjo, surrounded by a bunch of natives and tourists. They stopped awhile to talk with Kincaid and listen to him sing about mist-covered hills, and deep hidden stills, and dogwood blossoms and daffodils popping out in the spring back there in Tennessee.

A lot of times when we was underway, usually during the noon lunch break or in early evening when the crew gathered in small groups about the weather deck to discuss partying and women and home and all those thing sailors talk about, Kincaid would be there. He'd either be playing by himself for an appreciative audience or jamming with the ship's postal clerk on his mandolin and one of the quartermasters, who played one mean fiddle.

Everyone from the lowliest seaman recruit clear up to the captain enjoyed Kincaid's music. I was on the bridge the first time we refueled underway. As the tanker was hauling the hoses back to its deck, the skipper calls out to me, "Boatswain's Mate Morgan, get Kincaid up here quick and have him bring that banjo of his."

So, I get on the 1MC, mash down the button, give a blast of the pipe and call for "Seaman Apprentice Kincaid and his banjo, lay to the bridge on the double." That drew a bit of a laugh around ship but within minutes, here comes Kincaid, grinning and holding that old banjo.

"Kincaid," the Old Man says, "I want you to play us a breaking away song, and I want a lively one. Think you can do that, son?"

Kincaid grins, says, "Aye aye, sir." He walks over to where I'm holding out the 1MC button. The Old Man tells me, "Make sure that's on all circuits, Boatswain's Mate;" and I reply, "Aye aye, Skipper."

That's how, some 200 miles south southwest of Midway Island, as a Navy missile frigate pulled away at flank speed from a Navy tanker, the frantic happy sounds of a banjo drifted across the waters, painting a picture of wiry jockeys on race horses galloping around a dirt race track, going like the wind with a thundering of hooves. From then on, anytime we were finishing up an underway or vertical replenishment, as the distance widened between us and the oiler or the helicopter, the sounds of Kincaid's banjo came racing across and through the ship. Got us feeling even cockier than we already felt.

Kincaid drew other pictures for us with his playing – images of county seats on market day, and little one-horse towns on sleepy Saturday afternoons, and hoe-downs in lantern-lit barns on Saturday nights, and people walking to church on Sunday morning. The songs he played the most, though, and the ones we all liked the best, were the ones about the wives and girlfriends and mothers waiting back home. He sang about dark-eyed mountain gals walking barefoot along the side of the road, and young ladies with goldenrod hair flowing out from under gingham sun bonnets, and mothers rocking in a darkened room while they sang softly to the babies in their arms, and women with fire in their eyes dancing up a storm on an old plank floor, and grey-haired grandmothers in flour sack aprons cooking up a bubbling blend of fried chicken and green tomatoes on an old coal-fired cook stove.

Kincaid had a girl waiting for him, his high school sweetheart. Polly was her name, and he talked and sang about how they were going to be married once he finished his hitch on the Wolf and returned home to that little bungalow he had picked out on a pretty piece of wooded land with a creek babbling through. Seemed like every mailbag leaving the ship had a letter in it from him to her, and every mailbag that came back had a reply.

When we pulled into Subic Bay, Kincaid was one of those who remained true to his girl back home when more shipmates than I care to admit headed toward the pleasures of Olangapo City just outside the main gate. That sort of business works both ways, I guess. The term is "Westpac Widows," and describes the girlfriends and wives who find an extended separation too long. That's when the Dear John letters start coming in. Some shipmates reacted with anger, others with casual acceptance. Then there were the ones you thought their heart had been ripped out.

That's how Kincaid reacted when he got a letter from his gal saying she couldn't wait for him and had taken up with some other guy back there at home. From that day, he kept playing but not as much and the songs he did play got sadder and slower. He didn't sing about sun-speckled fields or puppies playing in the hay anymore. His songs were about thunderstorms in mountain passes and lonely old folks.

One evening when we were steaming through the Sea of Japan, Kincaid was by himself up in the bow, strumming idly on his guitar. The bow had always been a favorite place of that Tennessee backwoods boy because of the porpoises drawn by the sonar pinging; leaping through the waves alongside the ship, sometimes as many as a dozen or more of them, a whole school flying through the water. Now with that broken heart of his, he seemed to like the little bit of isolation up there in the bow even more.

The Old Man was prowling back and forth on the bridge that evening, which didn't go over too good with the rookie lieutenant who had the watch. We were looking out the windows down at Kincaid when he suddenly stopped playing, cried out like an animal that had been shot, and flung his guitar over the side. The Old Man stared down, whirled toward me and shouted, "Sound General Quarters, Bos'n! Man overboard! Mr. Parker, get this ship turned around!"

"Skipper," I said; "by the time we get back here, that guitar will be a hundred fathoms under."

He glared at me, then nodded his head. "You're right, Boats. Belay that order, Mr. Parker."

We looked out at Kincaid and he was just sitting there with his head down. Word travels fast through a Navy ship and that night, from fo'c'sle to fantail, things were as quiet as an off limits bar on a Sunday afternoon. If it's possible for 8,000 tons of steel to cry, the USS Wolf shed some tears that night as she plowed through the swells rolling across from China to Japan.

After that, Kincaid still played some on his banjo but his heart just wasn't in it anymore. We went on station with a carrier home ported in Sasebo and were involved in various multination exercises and had some good liberty in Bangkok and Singapore and a few other ports, and all in all it was a pretty decent cruise, but that little black cloud of Kincaid's girl dumping him kept hanging over the whole ship.

Time skims fast over the waves when about all you do is work and sleep with an occasional breather in port. We eventually set a course back east toward San Diego and the day finally came when we steamed under the green-covered bluffs of Point Loma, headed in toward the 34th Street naval station. I was on the starboard bridge wing when Chief Signalman McMyers called out for The Old Man to hustle back and take a look through the big eyes binoculars on the port side. I meandered back out of curiosity and was in time to see the skipper stand back up and holler at me, "Morgan! Get Kincaid up here on the double!"

Well, I passed the word, then took a look myself through the big eyes. There on one of the rusty tracks where they pushed out those big defense searchlights in World War II to shine down on the Japanese fleet that never did show up, was a homemade sign big as a billboard. On it were the words, "Troob, I love you. Please forgive me." And standing next to the sign was the figure of a girl in a flowered dress that swirled about in the wind blowing in from across the Pacific.

When Kincaid came topside, The Old Man had him take a look through the binoculars at the image we were gradually leaving behind. Kincaid stiffened, then looked up at the captain.

"Give her a chance, sailor," the skipper said in a soft voice. "Love and forgiveness; they go together like seagulls and blue sky."

Just then one of the deckhands from First Division came hauling up the portside ladder and he had Kincaid's banjo with him. The Old Man glanced over at me and I flipped the signal bridge 1MC on all circuits below decks and topside. Kincaid gave an embarrassed grin, walked over to where I was holding the mike, nodded his head, and I mashed down the button.

His fingers started flying across those banjo strings like they hadn't done in months. Music flowed into the warm air as we began our starboard swing around the channel past North Island. Sailboats and pleasure cruisers and expensive yachts and dinghies skimmed and scooted about the blue-green water to Kincaid's sounds of puppy dogs frolicking in barnyards and church youth groups picking blackberries and good old boys in feedlots laughing and joking. As we steamed under the sweeping curve of Coronado Bridge with boats pulling in alongside and behind us in a welcoming parade, the banjo music sang out about chess pies cooling on kitchen windowsills and quarter horses racing across sun-drenched pastures and storekeepers waiting on customers in stores with wooden plank floors and old folks coming out on the front porch to greet little grandkids toddling up the sidewalk.

When we finally pulled alongside the pier, there among the couple hundred or so wives and girlfriends and sons and daughters and moms and dads was the girl in the dress that swirled about in the wind. One thing, though. Up close alongside the pier, we saw what we hadn't made out through the binoculars looking up at the headland on Point Loma. That gal was obviously pregnant; and remember, we'd been gone for 11 months.

I heard later how one of the data systems technicians, a typical smart aleck OD Division type named Viss, was standing at the rail amidships and he made a comment that no gentleman should make about a lady. He happened to be standing next to Hull Technician Second Class Keller when he made that comment. Keller's nickname is "Forklift." He has to duck his head and turn sideways when he goes through a doorway. Forklift has fists the size of hams. He doesn't talk much and he didn't talk much then. He just sort of turned that tech toward him, sunk a right ham into his gut, snapped his head back with a left ham to the chin, and left him sprawled on the deck, counting gooney birds swirling in his head.

Troob Kincaid was one of the first ones down the gangplank once it was lowered and secured. We watched as he ran up to his Polly, slowed for a second as they looked at one another and spoke, and then gathered her into his arms. If they didn't set a record for the length of a kiss, they came mighty close.

As other sailors poured down the gangplank and rushed into the crowd, Kincaid and the girl he had come home to walked arm-in-arm down the pier, her head on his shoulder. Jimmy Maughan, the ship's corpsman, told some of the crew later down in sickbay how, just as Kincaid and Polly were walking under the dockside crane, the pigeons roosting up in its girders all seemed to freeze in place and bow their heads. Maughan has a bit of an imagination, so I don't know about that. Quite a few of us, though, did see something we'd never seen this close to land before. As Troop Kincaid and his Polly walked along in their own little world, several porpoises went arcing through the waters alongside the pier. The way they were grouped, it was almost like they were in formation, saluting someone or something.

Kincaid left the Wolf a few weeks later when his hitch was up. A couple months after that, Postal Clerk Lucindell, one of Troob's musical buddies he used to jam with, got a letter from Kincaid. Enclosed was a photo of him and Polly on the porch steps of a log cabin with flowers growing up the posts and a rocking chair next to a window that red checkered curtains were blowing through. Leaning up against the doorframe was a banjo and a guitar. Troob was holding a little baby and had a big grin on his face. Standing next to them, her hair kind of tousled as if by a breeze blowing through the dogwoods, was Polly. Her hand was on her husband's shoulder and she was looking at him and their little boy with an expression as loving as you've ever seen.

I signed up for another four-year hitch aboard. I like being at sea. I like the roll of the ship and the waves rushing by and the sun on the equator beating down on the steel missile houses and the swabbies in Deck Division during the day and the Southern Cross and the North Star glittering down on us at night as the Milky Way sweeps across the sky. Sometimes at night during the midwatch when the ship is rocking through the swells and the salt air is blowing across the weather decks and all you can see is the black outlines of the superstructure looming overhead and the radar dishes slowly turning, I can hear Troob Kincaid again, playing and singing about a little place alongside the Loosahatchie River, and a gal who could pull any sailor from the sea.

That boy, he didn't just play with heart alone, he played for two hearts intertwined.

# Dreams That from Cupid Fall Gently

*(The rock group Poco's song "Sagebrush Serenade" was one of the inspirations for this story. The following stanza especially stood out: "Who'd have thought you'd fall into my dreams. Turned around and there you were in cowboy boots and faded jeans." The other inspiration was the 1988 movie "The Milagro Beanfield War," based on a novel of the same name by John Nichols.)*

("Cupid, come here," commanded Gabriel.

The cherub flew to where the archangel was peering through the clouds. Gabriel stretched out his arm and pointed toward Earth.

"There are your next targets," he said. "His name is Morgan; a 15-year-old boy in a small town who hopes for love but thinks it has passed him by. Her name is Felicia, a 14-year-old daughter of migrant workers who recently settled in the community where Morgan's family lives. It has been decreed that they should fall in love. See to it."

Cupid checked his quiver to ensure he had sufficient arrows, tested the tautness of his bowstring, and sped down through the sky.)

Morgan wondered what was wrong with him. All of his buddies dated; a number of them even had girlfriends. He liked girls but the few who had interested him had rejected his clumsy overtures. While stocking the shelves in his family's hardware store, he would daydream of walking with a girl hand-in-hand along lamplit lanes. At night, the faces of anonymous girls floated through his dreams.

The first day of school after Christmas vacation, Morgan's math teacher, Mr. Nishimura, had just finished taking roll when a late student walked into the classroom and handed the teacher a note.

Morgan stared at the girl and felt as though a linebacker had just blindside-tackled him. He saw a vision with long black hair and dark eyes. Whereas slacks, blouses, skirts and dresses were the norm for the girls in school, this girl was wearing a plaid work shirt, faded jeans and cowboy boots.

Mr. Nishimura gazed around the classroom at the handful of empty seats. He glanced at Morgan, smiled, and told the girl, "Please take that seat over there; third row, fourth seat back."

Morgan continued staring at the girl as she sat down. She glanced his way, shot a look of disdain, and turned her attention to her notebook and what the teacher was saying. Morgan felt the familiar crush of rejection, mentally shrugged, and listened to Mr. Nishimura.

As Felicia took notes, she thought bitterly to herself that this was the seventh school she had attended in three years. The migrant life isn't designed to help the social life of adolescents. She thought of her amigas back in Ciudad Juarez, and the fiestas and carnavales they would have been enjoying over the just finished season of Navidad.

Thus began Morgan's daily anguish and Felicia's daily frustration. The more he saw of this girl, the more he fell in love. The more she felt his moonstruck glances directed her way, the more she ignored him.

The upcoming 4-H show helped divert Morgan's attention. He hadn't tried out for the basketball team this year in order to concentrate on a sheep he was raising on his grandfather's farm at the outskirts of town. With Gramps' help, he was sure Harvey was a blue ribbon winner gazing up at him whenever he entered the pen to feed and water the snowy animal. Morgan would tend to Harvey but his mind would be on the girl who sat next to him in math class.

Felicia too was raising a sheep to enter in the 4-H show. Her father's sister, Tia Consuela, was a member of the extended family that had settled

– for how long, they weren't sure – in the community. Tia Consuela saw and understood her young niece's frustration at having to sacrifice the traditional pleasures of a teen for the economic reality of farm laborers. Consuela knew the benefits that come with being responsible for an animal, and the joy and pride that accompany recognition of that animal. It had been difficult convincing her hardheaded niece to take on the challenge. In the end, though, Felicia had grudgingly agreed to care for the sheep her aunt had bought at a local market. The girl called the animal Blancocita.

One evening in February, a restless Morgan put on his football sweats and went out for a jog. His homework was finished, Harvey had received his daily care, and the youth was working to maintain his football conditioning until track season started. Also, he needed to stay active to keep his mind off the girl who sat next to him in math class – the vision who continued to scorn his every attempt to strike up a conversation.

He was running past a fenced lot when he heard a sudden, high-pitched baaing. In the light of the three-quarters moon, he saw several upright, shadowy shapes striking out at an animal huddled in a corner. He caught a few snatches of hoarse, low shouts – "Stupid pepperbelly sheep!" and "Make it scream louder!"

"Hey!" Morgan scrambled over the fence and sprinted toward the attackers. They whirled toward him, then rushed at him. He lashed out and knocked down two of them but the others struck him to the ground, kicked him several times, and in an instant the group was outside the fence and running down the road out of sight.

Morgan got slowly to his feet and hobbled over to where the animal lay. He knelt and reached out when the porch light at a nearby mobile home came on, bathing him in light. The boy stood just as a girl darted out on the porch. It was Felicia.

He realized later he should have stayed and tried to explain to the girl. However, when she came rushing through the fence waving a flashlight, shined it on her prize sheep and Morgan, and began striking out at him, his only instinct was to turn and run.

The following day at school, Felicia's seat was empty. The next day she returned. As the girl took her place, her glare seared through Morgan and he winced when she hissed, "Criminal! Bestia!"

She would have no more to do with him. Over the next week, Morgan used the small town grapevine to learn that Blancocita would recover. However, the broken leg the sheep had suffered would keep it from the upcoming 4-H competition.

One evening, Morgan approached his father reading in the living room.

"Dad, can you drive me over to a friend's house so I can drop off something?"

Mr. Johnson smiled. His son was a good kid and he was willing to humor the boy's occasional unusual requests, no questions asked.

"Sure, son. Let me get my coat and keys."

Morgan directed his father the several miles to the mobile home adjacent to the pen where Blancocita lay recuperating in a hay-filled shed. He walked up the porch stairs and was about to leave a note on the door when it opened. It was Felicia. He started to hand her the note but she lashed out and struck it to the ground. A torrent of Spanish the boy didn't understand flew about his ears but there was no mistaking the meaning. He turned and fled back to the car as the girl slammed the door behind her.

Mr. Johnson stared at his son. The boy looked over at his father. A tear ran down Morgan's cheek.

"Daddy!" he blurted out and the two reached for one another. As the father hugged his son to him, he thought how Morgan had not called him "Daddy" in years.

"I love you, Morgan," was all the man could think to say as he held his the boy.

When they arrived home, Morgan ran upstairs while Mr. Johnson explained what he knew to his waiting wife.

A gust of wind swept through the town about that time. It swirled around a mobile home, scooped up the note Felicia had knocked from Morgan's hand, and sent the piece of paper fluttering across the ground to the base of a telephone pole. A figure emerged from the shadows, reached down and picked up the note. The feeble flame of a lighter cast its light onto the following, neatly printed words: "Felicia. I was not trying to hurt your sheep. I was trying to protect it from some guys who were kicking it. I'm sorry it's busted up too bad to be in the 4-H competition. I want to give you my sheep so that way you can still enter. I'll bet he wins you a prize. I'll bring his papers to school tomorrow. Sincerely, Morgan Johnson. P.S. I sit next to you in math class."

The figure folded back the note and stood looking first at the nearby pen, then at the mobile home. Miguel, El Rey de Carora, was a figure well known to both the Hispanic and the Anglo communities. He shuffled about town in his patched and frayed clothes, doing odd jobs to earn enough change to buy his meager food and maintain the shack in which he lived a solitary existence. He thought about the note and remembered long ago in the foothills of Baja California when a senorita had spurned his advances. He recalled how a week before he had been standing in almost this same spot when he had seen a young boy hurdle the fence and race to the rescue of Felicia Gonzalez' pet sheep. Miguel walked toward the light shining from the mobile home.

A half hour later, the phone rang at the Johnson residence. Mrs. Johnson answered and listened for several minutes. She called her husband to the phone and he too listened for a long time. He thanked the caller, hung up, and smiled at his wife.

"Well, want to flip a coin to see who has to go get their coat and the car keys?"

"First we need to go tell Morgan."

When the car pulled up in front of the mobile home, the porch light illuminated a young girl in a coat waiting on the porch swing.

"Felicia's aunt said she would bring you home, son."

"OK, Mom," the boy replied as he got out of the car. He looked back in and smiled at her.

"Thanks, Mom. I love you."

"I love you too, son."

The car pulled away into the fresh night air as Morgan walked up the porch stairs and took the seat Felicia offered next to her on the swing. They talked for several minutes in hushed voices, the girl speaking urgently, the boy more shyly.

Then, on that late winter evening, a skyful of stars twinkling down

86

on them, a young boy and girl sitting on a porch swing shared that first, innocent, magical kiss.

("Cupid, you have done well," said the archangel Gabriel.

The cherub looked embarrassed.

"Your eminence," he replied, "I did nothing. My bowstring broke on the journey to Earth. I was no more than an observer."

The archangel frowned. "Then who … ?"

The two of them glanced down through the clouds together. Smiles of understanding spread across their faces.

"There are our cupids," Gabriel said. "A math teacher, a boy's grandfather, a girl's aunt, a mother and father, an opportune gust of wind, and a lonely old man considered 'loco' by the townspeople."

"Don't forget the roles Harvey and Blancocita played," Cupid said.

Gabriel chuckled. "Yes, Cupid; love is capable of spreading its wings in many wondrous ways.")

❤ ❤ ❤

# EASTER

✝ ✝ ✝

# Why a Rabbit Delivers Easter Eggs

(Only a few jellybeans and a strawberry crème egg remained in the plastic grass. The child studied the basket, frowned, set it on the porch steps, and toddled over to his grandfather's racking chair.

"Granpaw, why isn't it an Easter chicken?"

The old man had nodded off in the early afternoon sun and his head jerked up. "Eh, what's that, boy?"

"Why is it an Easter rabbit? Eggs come from chickens, not rabbits, Why isn't it an Easter chicken?"

The old man scratched behind his ear, then reached for the child. "Hop up here, boy. Let me tell you a story about why that is.")

Once upon a time, many years ago and in a land far away, lived two friends – a rabbit and a chicken. The rabbit's name was Ezekiel. The chicken's name was Rebecca. Now, it might seem strange that two animals so different would be friends. Remember, though, that this was at a time when the world was more innocent. It was a simpler place to live then.

Ezekiel lived with his relatives in an expanse of rocks and bushes near the small village where Rebecca resided with the rest of a small flock in a coop behind their owners' cottage. On most days when it wasn't raining – and it seldom rained in the land where these friends lived – Ezekiel would hop the short distance to the coop. Rebecca would strut out to meet him and the two would pass most of the day strolling about the landscape, searching for sweet grasses for the rabbit and bugs and grain for the chicken, and taking long naps on outcrops of rock warmed by the sun.

Both were simple but curious animals and they would talk for hours about the change of seasons, what they saw in both the day and the night sky, the behavior of the humans in the village, and the merits and characteristics of various animals.

One day Ezekiel, the more adventuresome of the two friends, convinced Rebecca they should take a short journey to see what lay in the desert to the east. They made a strange pair moving across the land. Ezekiel would hop for a long distance and then wait while Rebecca, who alternated between trotting and half flying with frantically flapping wings, would hurry to catch up. This difference in traveling style was more than compensated for by what the two animals shared: a deep friendship and affection for one another, and a curiosity as to what lay over the next ridge.

Two mornings after they had left the village behind, they came upon a man sitting on the ground, leaning against a large boulder. They hopped and fluttered closer. The man was barefoot and dressed in a simple robe. His shoulder length hair was matted with perspiration and he was breathing heavily. He glanced up as they approached and smiled. Ezekiel and Rebecca looked into the kindest eyes they had ever seen. Although the man's face was pale and shaken, he spoke to them in a gentle voice.

"Hello, little friends. Have you come to help me overcome the effects of my trial and temptation?"

Instinctively, Ezekiel hopped into the man's arms and felt the warmth he was sharing come flowing back to him ten-fold. Rebecca sensed the moment was right for her morning laying, and so produced one of her fine, large, brown eggs.

"And how did you know, feathered one, that I have not eaten these 40 days and so am famished?" The man picked up the egg, cracked it, and swallowed the contents. The color came back to his face, he gave Ezekiel a final hug and placed him on the ground, and rose to his feet.

"I thank you, simple creatures, for your comfort and nourishment. And now I must be on my way. I have my father's work to continue." He reached down to scratch Ezekiel behind the ears and ruffle the feathers around Rebecca's neck. "I think we will meet again." he said.

The man picked up a heavy tree branch that lay nearby, snapped off both ends as though they were mere twigs, and strolled off to the west. He turned once to wave goodbye to the two animals. Ezekiel stood on his hind feet and his nose twitched. Rebecca clucked and ruffled her feathers. The two friends watched until the man was out of sight, then talked excitedly about what had taken place. They both felt as though somehow their journey had reached a climax, and so it was time to return home.

Back in the village, many months passed. One day Ezekiel and Rebecca were on their favorite outcrop of rock overlooking the village when a small band of men walked into the settlement and seated themselves in a grove of olive trees. Even from a distance away, both animals realized the leader of this group resting in the hot sun was their friend from the desert.

Excited, they hopped and fluttered down to the village and across the dusty street toward where the men were sipping water. A boy, seeing the rabbit, took up a stone and threw it. The missile struck Ezekiel in his hindquarters and he cried with pain. The lad picked up another stone but Rebecca threw herself at the attacker, flapping her wings, pecking and squawking. The youth, astonished, fled down an alley. Rebecca returned to her friend, only to find that the man had picked up the rabbit.

Ezekiel felt his pain vanish as the fingers stroked his fur. The man looked about the crowd that had gathered, at members of his own group and villagers.

"A good man takes care of his animals but wicked men are cruel to theirs," he said in a voice that flowed like a mountain spring. One of the townswomen came up to the group dragging by the ear the boy who had cast the stone. The man motioned for the woman to release the boy. "Hate not the sinner but rather the sin," he said quietly.

The man stooped down, placed Ezekiel next to the waiting Rebecca, and looked into their eyes. "I think we will meet one more time," he said with a sad smile.

The travelers continued on their way. Life in the village returned to regular routine. The months passed. One night Ezekiel heard Rebecca calling to him from outside his warren. He squirmed to the surface to find her pacing back and forth.

"The man is in danger!" she said. "I feel it. We must go to him."

Because his feathered friend had willingly gone upon the journey he had suggested many months before, Ezekiel readily agreed to travel now on this pilgrimage she insisted upon. Their odyssey took them from a landscape of few and scattered settlements to more and larger villages. One day they saw on a plain before them a great city.

Rebecca suddenly settled in the shelter of a stone wall and cried out to Ezekiel. "I can go no farther," she said. "I am older than you and have reached the limit of my endurance. You much go on for both of us. But here," and she nudged outward with her beak a large brown egg. "Take this to the man for me. I must stay here."

Ezekiel protested at leaving his friend behind but she insisted. Gingerly taking the egg in his mouth, he rubbed his fur against the down on her neck, then turned and sped on toward a hill in the city where he saw activity.

Storm clouds gathered overhead and rain began to pelt the little rabbit as he dashed from one shelter to the next. With a final rush of speed he burst through a final maze of houses and walls onto the top of the hill. Hunkering down against the wind and the rain, the egg still held in his mouth, he could only stare at the scene before him.

Three large wooden crosses stood on the hill. Two strangers were tied to the smaller crosses but in the center cross, Ezekiel saw the man who had befriended Rebecca and him, his arms stretched out onto the crossbeam. The rabbit looked with horror at the blood that oozed from wounds in the man's hands and feet where nails protruded, nails driven through the man's flesh into the wood.

The rabbit's mouth fell open, letting the egg slip onto the ground, where it smashed and oozed out its contents.

"Oh, friend!" he said sadly.

The man's eyes had been closed but he opened them now and looked down upon the trembling animal and the broken egg. The man's mouth moved and Ezekiel read the words. "My friends. You have brought me a gift. I thank you."

But then the man's back arched outward in pain and he lifted his face to the sky and called, "My God, my God, why hast thou forsaken me?" His head fell forward then, and he was still.

Ezekiel could only stare at the scene before him. "Oh, master!" he cried. For the first time in his life, the rabbit wept, and his tears poured like the rain that was flooding down around him.

Ezekiel turned and fled blindly into the storm. He stumbled under the shelter of some bushes. Exhaustion and grief sent him into a long deep sleep.

He awakened to a dancing breeze and a sweet blue sky. Looking out from his shelter, he saw the man, now dressed in a brilliant white robe, stooped down looking at him. On the man's shoulder perched Rebecca. She clucked when she saw her friend.

The man reached out to Ezekiel, who hopped into the hands he held out – hands unblemished from any injuries. The man rubbed his cheek against Ezekiel's soft fur. The rabbit trembled with excitement and Rebecca clucked and clucked.

"The two of you came to me twice in times of need and tended to me," the man said. "The first egg nourished my stomach; the second, my spirit. From henceforth, I say to you, the anniversary of this day shall be celebrated as a time of birth and renewal by the distribution of colorfully painted eggs and treats to the little children. The eggs, Rebecca, will be yours. The means of delivering them will be through you, Ezekiel."

The man placed the two friends back on the ground, gave them both a final pat, then strolled through the trees. Just before he disappeared, he turned and spread his arms, palms outward, toward the animals. The rabbit and the chicken found themselves back on their favorite rock perch overlooking the little village.

They continued their daily meetings and discussions although now they had a great deal more to discuss and wonder over.

The months passed, and the years, and the decades, and the centuries. Today, every Easter, descendants of Ezekiel are known collectively as The Easter Bunny. They deliver to the children eggs provided by the descendants of Rebecca.

And that is why rabbits deliver the Easter eggs.

(The little boy sat up from where he had been resting his head on his grandfather's shirt.

"I like that story,Granpaw," he said.

"I'm glad, young fella," the old man said. "Keep it in mind the next time you're chowing down on all that candy. Now go find me some jellybeans. I've worked up an appetite. Easter isn't just for you young'uns, you know.")

# HALLOWEEN

# The Specter by the Woodpile

*(The song "Africa" by the rock group Toto inspired me to write both a poem and the following story. A number of interpretations have been offered for the lyrics of "Africa." My interpretation centers on a man who sets out on a seemingly impossible journey in order to be reunited with the one he loves.)*

Memories of the old woman and the woodpile had haunted the traveler for a year. Now, he had returned to the Midsouth. His car bounced along the same dirt land he had driven down twice the previous October – once by accident, the second time on purpose to see for himself what he found it difficult to believe.

The ruts seemed deeper this time. Dead tree limbs littered the way, and vines snaked in from the undergrowth on either side of the lane. Overgrown bushes scraped against the sides of his car. The first two times, the going had been smoother, leaving him that much more unprepared for what he would find deep in this thick wood along the Loosahatchie River bottoms.

He had made a wrong turn that first time, winding up in the front yard of a shotgun house set in a small clearing. An old woman wearing a calico dress sat on the porch cracking walnuts. She gave him directions to where he needed to go, then offered him some iced tea. She rose slowly from her rocker and walked into the dim interior of the house. Her gray hair woven in two long braids hung down over a white lace shawl.

He was wiping his brow with his handkerchief when she came back out and handed him an aluminum tumbler. She eased back down in her chair as he drank. "Doesn't seem to make sense that the last day October should be so warm," he said between sips. She smiled at him, her piercing blue eyes twinkling from a face leathery and wrinkled. "A lot of the good Lord's works don't make sense to us, young man," she said. "But things always work out in the end."

The traveler glanced up at the chimney poking above the shingle roof. "Do you heat by wood?" he asked. The old woman nodded. He glanced around. A few logs lay scattered on the ground between rows of stakes he recognized as the end supports for a woodpile. "If you don't mind my asking, aren't you cutting it a bit close to lay in a supply before winter?"

The old woman turned her head and gazed at the pile. "My husband always provides for me," she said in a quiet voice. She seemed lost in thought for a moment, then suddenly looked at the traveler and smiled again. "When he proposed to me, that was one of the promises he made. Tonight, the wood will be here, as always."

The traveler sensed a desire in the old woman to tell him more, and he listened as she told her tale. She talked of their years together during the Depression, of his going off to sea when U.S. convoys began fighting their way across the North Atlantic, carrying troops and supplies to the Allies.

Before her husband left, he had already cut enough wood for her first winter alone. However, with the approach of her second winter without him, she had managed to accumulate only a small amount of wood as the cold winter nights howled closer.

One night, she heard a series of strange sounds outside. She took a kerosene lantern and her husband's shotgun and walked onto the porch. All she could see were bare treetops whipping in the wind. The next morning, she found rows of neatly split and stacked logs stretching across the length of the yard – enough wood to last through winter.

"Six days later, one of the boys from town brought me a telegram," she said. "It was from the War Department. My husband's ship had been torpedoed off the coast of Greenland a week before, and there were no survivors."

The traveler started to speak but she continued. "I remembered then what he had told me on our wedding day, that he had never loved anyone as much as he loved me, and nothing would ever keep us apart." She looked down at her hands lying motionless on the bowl of walnuts. "'Nothing,' he said, 'not even death.'"

The traveler felt a shiver run down his back. The old woman saw his reaction and smiled at him warmly. "Every year since then, I've walked out on the porch the morning of the day after the ship went down, and the supply of firewood for winter is there in the yard. Several years early on, I tried waiting outside, but something drew me back in the house, something that said it just couldn't happen while I was there; not while we're in different worlds."

The traveler hadn't known what to say, so he had thanked the old woman for the tea and left. He recalled what she had said, that "Tonight, the wood will be here." The next morning, before moving on to his next destination, he found his way back to the lane in the woods. He drove into the yard and saw the rows of firewood piled in neat stacks across the yard. The old woman heard his car and came to the door. She nodded as if to say she understood his need to come back and see for himself. They waved to one another, and he continued on his journey.

Now it was one year later, to the day. For the third time, he was driving down the lane to the house in the woods. He had had a long day, and the full moon was already low on the horizon when he reached the house. He shut off the engine and stared. The roof had collapsed and the chimney lay toppled in the weeds. The remains of a trash fire formed a blackened circle at the base of the steps. The screen door dangled on one hinge. He got out of his car and walked to where the woodpile had been, to where it should be again. The ground was bare.

"I'm sorry," the traveler whispered, and walked back to his car. He was about to start the engine when, through the wind, he thought he heard someone whisper, "Don't be sorry."

Glancing back toward where he had seen the final woodpile, he saw them standing there, a man and a woman, shimmering in the moonlight.

The man wore the uniform of a sailor. He had his arm around a woman wearing a calico dress. Her long hair hung down over a white lace shawl.

The reunited couple faded into the moonlight, but not before the woman smiled at the traveler. Through the darkness, her piercing blue eyes twinkled like twin stars.

# THE PUMPKIN MAN

It was a night painted in black and shades of gray, with an occasional splotch of orange and red. Clouds scurried across the sky and spat down an occasional raindrop. The moon cast its light through bare branches tossed about by the wind, sending shadows twisting across the sidewalk like tentacles. Miniature ghosts, ballerinas, pirates and devils gripped their bags as they scampered through the neighborhoods.

Skeletons dancing in the wind, jack-o-lanterns illuminated by flickering flames, and scarecrows stuffed for the occasion, were the doormen who greeted the trick-or-treaters as they ran up porch stairs. Grownups relegated to candy duty acted as maitre d's, and candy bars and bubble gum highlighted the menu specials. A hurried thank you, and the little customers became lawn shadows cast by streetlights as they moved on to the next house.

Only a handful visited a house that loomed up from a tangle of bushes and overgrown gardens on a corner lot. This was the house of The Pumpkin Man. The children never said his name aloud. They whispered it, since no one knew the true powers of The Pumpkin Man.

His was a reputation that had grown in the three years since he moved to the town. The name hand-painted on his mailbox read simply "Prometheus," which added to the children's wonderment. Someone said The Pumpkin Man had lived in the mountains of Tibet and learned strange powers there. Someone else heard that he had grown up in a gypsy circus that traveled through Eastern Europe, and had developed the ability to perform magic.

The Pumpkin Man grew a variety of vegetables and fruits, which he sold to local grocers. His specialty, though, was pumpkins. That was how he acquired his nickname. He could be seen tending to his special crop at all hour. More than one person had witnessed a dark shape moving among the vines in the dead of night.

That his was an appropriate nickname became clear the first Halloween after The Pumpkin Man moved to town. The older children who were brave enough to go to his door, and the few younger ones who accepted the dares of their friends, were greeted by a costumed figure dressed in rags, leather gloves on his hands, and a jack-o-lantern for a head. The Pumpkin Man even appeared to have a lighted candle in the carved pumpkin so its smiling face glowed down at the startled youngsters. Many of the children, when they saw this apparition towering over them, bolted down the steps back to the safety of the sidewalk. Those who stayed always received a large red apple.

The Pumpkin Man never spoke a word to the trick-or-treaters. He would bend at the waist, drop an apple in each bag, straighten, wait for the children to leave, then turn and walk back into the house.

This had been the pattern during the first two Halloweens that The Pumpkin Man had lived there. Some of the children said the apples were poisoned and threw them away. Those who ate the fruit were none the worse, though a few claimed they had nightmares afterward.

The grownups who paid any attention to the commotion over The Pumpkin Man told the children to stop acting so foolishly. They said he was an old man who simply wanted to be left alone but who was willing to be kind to them on Halloween.

On this third Halloween, one of the older boys decided not to leave well enough alone. He accepted his apple from The Pumpkin Man, then lagged behind as the rest of his group ran back to the sidewalk. In their excitement, and with the wind blowing leaves and raindrops about them, they didn't notice when he slipped away and hid in the shadow of a large pine tree. He looked up and down the street to be sure no other trick-or-treaters were near, then ran up to the porch, rang the bell, and hurried back to the safety of the tree.

The door opened and The Pumpkin Man stepped onto the porch. His jack-o-lantern head slowly swiveled from one side to the other. The youngster grasped the apple, reared back, and threw as hard as he could.

He had meant to hit The Pumpkin Man in the chest. Instead, he was horrified to see the apple strike The Pumpkin Man's head. The jack-o-lantern jerked backward and fell to the porch floor with a wet thud. The rag-clothed figure, now without a head, swayed back and forth. To the youngster's horror, The Pumpkin Man pitched forward onto the boards and lay still.

The boy was frozen to the spot and for several seconds could only stare at the motionless figure in the dim glow of the porch light. He turned and ran out of the yard and down the street. He didn't visit any more houses that night, and never did tell anyone what he had done. It was a secret he took to his grave.

After the boy had disappeared down the street, the door of The Pumpkin Man's house swung open. The old man who walked out shook his head at the lifeless pile of rags and the shattered pumpkin. He carefully pushed the jack-o-lantern to one side of the porch and scooped up the rags in his arms. He glanced out at the empty street, then turned and carried the clothing back into the house. The door swung shut behind him.

Inside the house, he carried his bundle down creaking stairs to the basement. He walked through several rooms to a small door, unlocked it, and carried the rags inside. Turning on an overhead light bulb, he set the lifeless shape in a chair, rearranged the arms and legs to a more natural position, then turned to his workbench. He worked quickly, scooping out another pumpkin and carving a face on it. Once he was satisfied with his handiwork, he carried the jack-o-lantern over to the seated figure and planted it firmly on the shoulders.

The old man began chanting in a language from a faraway land. The inside of the pumpkin began glowing. Gradually the arms and legs began to fill out again. The old man watched as the figure stood and waited for his command.

"Come," he said with a smile. The figure followed the old man as he walked through the door toward the cellar stairs. "We still might have more visitors. They would be disappointed if they didn't receive their treat from The Pumpkin Man."

# Widow Gray's Halloween Surprise

Widow Gray had decided she would no longer put up with the Halloween pranks of those rapscallions.

For eight years, ever since Rufus had passed away in 1895, those rascals had evidently decided a widow woman living alone was a fine target for their Halloween orneriness.

Every October 31 it was something new. One year they had dismantled her buggy and re-assembled it on top of the goat shed. Another year, the pranksters took apart her rail fence and laid the rails across the road, creating a jarring series of bumps for unsuspecting wagons that came along early next morning.

A tipped over outhouse, water pails and milk jugs left hanging in trees, a plow sitting on the front porch – these were just a few of the surprises waiting for her the morning after Halloween night. On several occasions, she had cowered terrified while ghostly figures circled the house, wailing and knocking on the windows and walls.

This year, though, would be different. Widow Gray would teach those boys the lesson of their lives.

She made her preparations with care. To avoid attracting attention, she bought what she needed at several different stores. She even rode her wagon to nearby towns where she wasn't known, to make several purchases.

The widow began preparing her surprise in mid October. On Halloween Day, she stayed busy with final preparations in the barn. She had thought about setting up her surprise in her bungalow but she was a fussy housekeeper and would not be able to tolerate the mess that her surprise was bound to create. No, better to do it in the barn, with its straw and dirt floor.

That night, she sat down to wait in the darkest corner just inside the front door. Rufus' old double-barreled shotgun sat by her side.

The clock on the mantel had just struck half past 11 when she saw dark shapes flitting down the lane. The shapes huddled just outside the front gate, then broke up and went in different directions. Some headed toward the pasture; others slipped down either side of and behind the house.

Widow Gray slowly stood, clutching the shotgun. She leaned forward against the screen door, straining to hear above the wind and the branches rattling in the trees. She could make out but couldn't recognize distant muted sounds. She kept listening. In the den, the clock chimed 12 times. Midnight. It was time. She hefted the shotgun and eased out the door.

At that moment, behind the house, Vodie Kelley and two other boys were well on the way to finishing their assigned task. As Vodie toiled, he thought about the discussion earlier in the week in which the group had agreed to do something completely different to surprise Widow Gray.

Vodie's axe flashed down on the foot-long length of oak, neatly splitting it in two. Nearby, Whit Myers was wielding his axe with equal energy. The two kept Herb Sanders hopping, picking up the split wood and piling it neatly under the overhang of the wagon shed.

Shadows scurrying around the year showed where Glenn Winfrey, Tommy Parks and Pat Graves were picking up branches and sticks, breaking them into more manageable lengths, and stacking them by the back door in a steadily growing pile of kindling.

Farther out from the house, Jerry Wardlaw and Mike Gresham had almost completed their circuit of the pasture. They had found several gaps in the fence to mend, re-tacking wire to posts and re-sinking fallen posts.

It was Tommy Parks in the corner of the front yard who Widow Gray first spied and approached. Tommy heard the distinctive double click of a shotgun being cocked. The pale light from the cloud-shrouded, full moon illuminated the barrels aimed at his stomach.

"Not a word, sonny," Widow Gray hissed. "Turn around and walk toward the barn, real slow."

The other two boys were too busy to notice the pair walking in the dark toward the barn door. They heard Tommy call out softly, "Hey, fellas! Come over here quick!" without noticing the strange catch in his voice.

Glenn and Pat were the first ones to hear and hustle over to the side of the barn. They pulled up short when they found themselves facing the business end of a shotgun.

Widow Gray hissed more instructions, and this time it was Glenn who called out in a loud voice, "Hey, Vodie! Whit! Herb! Come over here, fast!"

Out in the pasture a short distance away, Jerry and Mike heard Glenn call out. Curious as to what was going on, they slipped under the fence and trotted across the yard. They too came to a sudden halt when they saw Widow Gray swinging a shotgun back and forth between them and their friends.

"Widow Gray! Wait a …" Glenn tried to explain. He was cut short by the widow making a stabbing motion toward him with the shotgun she held.

"Inside the barn, all of you," she snarled in a voice that sounded surprisingly strong for an elderly woman.

Slowly, the eight boys, thoroughly cowed by the unexpected appearance in the night of the widow, and the knowledge of what a double-barreled shotgun could do, shuffled into the dark, still interior of the barn. Widow Gray followed them and slid the door shut with a loud bang.

"Before we light the lantern, I just want you boys to know that I got plenty tired of your ornery tricks every Halloween. This year, I vowed I'd turn the tables on all of you. Jerry, yonder by where you're a'standin' is a lantern on a table, with a box of matches. You light up that lantern now."

The wind rattled the barn's doors and shutters as Jerry, his hands shaking, reached out in the dark and lit the wick of the kerosene lantern. The flame flared up in the glass chimney, its light revealing the surprise that the widow had toiled for two weeks to prepare.

Along one wall was a makeshift table made of several 2x8 boards laid on sawhorses. On the table were several plates heaped with pyramids of doughnuts. On either side of the doughnuts were several apple and pumpkin pies. Plates of Widow Gray's homemade fudge and oatmeal cookies sat alongside plates, forks and drinking mugs. Two soup ladles lay next to a pair of stone crocks from which the aroma of apple cider wafted outward.

The boys stared, their mouths hanging open. They all let out a collective, deep sigh of relief.

"Every Halloween you young'uns have done somethin' ornery to me," the widow said. "And every year I stewed and muttered and grumbled. Well, this year, I decided I'd do somethin' different.

"What y'all have done is downright mean but I got to thinkin' it ain't really been destructive, just mischievous. And, just a'playin' pranks don't mean y'all are bad boys. So, here's a Halloween treat for you, and I want you to dig in and help yourselves."

The eight lads looked at all the food and at one another, let out a whoop, and rushed toward the feast awaiting them. Widow Gray lit several more kerosene lanterns, turning what had been a dim, gloomy interior into a jolly, well-lit party scene.

She walked over to Whit Myers, who wasn't letting a mouthful of doughnut prevent him from gulping down his second mug of cider.

"Now tell me, you young whippersnapper," the widow said. "What devilry did y'all do tonight?"

Several of the boys started laughing as Herb slid open the heavy barn door. He motioned the widow over and waved a hand toward the pile of kindling by her back door, and the stack of firewood by the wagon shed.

"And Jerry and Mike got your fence fixed good and tight for the winter so you don't gotta worry 'bout those cows of yours gettin' out," he chuckled.

Widow Gray didn't know whether to laugh or cry.

"Ma'am, I gotta tell you, though," Pat said. "Maybe we fooled you by decidin' to do somethin' nice this year 'stead of somethin' ornery, but you shore snookered us, first with that shotgun, and then with all this great food."

Widow Gray turned and looked at the group of boys munching and drinking their fill. She suddenly swung the shotgun toward them, pulling first one trigger, then the other.

The boys froze but the only sound was a pair of clicks on empty chambers.

Another collective sigh of relief came from the group as the widow cackled and said, "Doughnuts are a whole lot nicer than buckshot, ain't they, boys? Y'all eat up now, and a happy Halloween to you!"

# Summertime

# The Day Big Dietrich Taught
# The Town A Lesson

Out in the fields, the mid-day sun beat down on rows of corn. High overhead, in a cloudless sky, a hawk drew lazy spirals as it passed by. A patch of sunlight poked through the motionless cottonwood branches onto a drooping rose bush at the foot of the porch steps. The only sound was the rhythmic squeaking of the porch swing's chains as the old man slowly rocked back and forth, back and forth, back and forth.

On the top step of the porch, the boy leaned forward from a post he was using as a backrest and his fingers stopped picking at the tangle of fishing line. For a long moment, he watched the twitching legs of the hound sleeping beneath the swing.

"Granpaw?"

The old man's head jerked up. He blinked his eyes and looked over at the steps. "What is it, boy?"

"I bet a rabbit could jump up and down in front of ol' Homer and he'd just let it be. He's lazy, that dog."

The old man frowned and looked at the hound. He reached down and patted a bony paw. The dog shifted its legs and began snoring. The old man stroked its head, then sat back up and looked at the boy.

"You best not be judging Homer by his looks, boy. It's a common enough mistake among folks. Reminds me of Big Dietrich. The whole dang town was wrong on him."

The boy felt a story coming and put aside the snarl of fishing line. He looked at his grandfather expectantly. The old man gazed out over the rows of corn and began his tale.

"It woulda been back around the summer of 1910 or '11, a few years before The Great War. I was a whippersnapper 'bout your age. Family of German immigrants moved into the old Adams place a mile up the road from my daddy's farm. Worked like beavers - fixed up all the barns and cleared out the brush and planted cotton and soybeans and corn.

"We'd pass 'em on the road ever so often; pleasant folks who spoke English with that strong accent, you know. Old Man and Old Lady Kleinmann and their daughter, Greta, a big gal with a round fact; and their two sons, Otto and Dietrich. Otto was a tall lanky fella, always whistling under his breath.

"Dietrich, though, we never could figure out why he was the way he was. Scowl on his face, eyebrows beaded together like two hairy lightning bolts, a mouth clamped together tighter'n a snapping turtle on a broomstick. And big! Lordy, he looked to weigh as much as the wagon he rode in. Roll him into a ball and toss him into the woods and he'd come nigh to knockin' over three kinds of oak trees. We could talk to the others on the road or in town, but Big Dietrich, as folks came to call him, we steered clear of.

"Wasn't we surprised, then, when word got around that Big Dietrich was courtin' Diney Sue, a little gal that wasn't the best lookin' filly in the area, but weren't the worst either, by a long shot. Folks figured she was a bit loco to give any encouragement to Big Dietrich, but figured too that was her business, and went about their own.

"Then one Saturday evening at the supper table, my daddy told of what he'd heard in town that day. Seems that several fellas of a rougher sort decided they didn't take to a 'foreigner' calling on Diney Sue, so four of 'em got together and jumped Big Dietrich on the edge of town. The way my daddy heard, all four of 'em were in a makeshift hospital that Doc Hatcher, who was also the town barber and dentist, set up in Tom O'Malley's Livery. All four was busted up pretty good. Big Dietrich, my daddy said, was in the town jail. Sheriff Cannon said he had to stay there until the circuit judge came through a week next Tuesday.

"Well, talk about a gathering 10 days later. Folks that shoulda been in their fields and shops and homes and school was packed into that little courtroom 'til it was fit to busting down the walls. I was there, playing hooky and hiding behind a post in the back corner. The sheriff brought in Big Dietrich in irons and then the four fellas that jumped him was brought in on stretchers, all bandaged up and their arms and legs sticking out in different directions in plaster of Paris casts. He done a real number on them boys.

"Judge Samuels had a reputation as a rough judge, and even though Big Dietrich's lawyer – who run one of the town's two mills – pleaded self defense, the condition of that sorry four made it look bad for Dietrich. His parents and Greta and Otto sat up front looking miserable, and Old Lady Kleinmann weeping into a handkerchief. Big Dietrich just growled his replies to questions put to him, and looked meaner than ever.

"Then it happened. The prosecutor – some fancy pants lawyer from the county seat – asked Big Dietrich how he felt about what he done. At first, Dietrich glared at him. Then, he got a strange expression and looked down and his shoulders began to shake. The whole courtroom was death quiet as everyone stared. Big Dietrich was crying.

"He looked up, tears runnin' down his cheeks, and he blurted out, 'I'm scar't.'

"Judge Samuels looked at Big Dietrich and said, 'Young man, why are you scared?'

"Big Dietrich just shook his head and bowed it down, but the judge said again in a louder voice, 'Mr. Kleinmann, what are you scared of?'

"Dietrich lifted his head again, peered around the courtroom like he was lookin' for someone, then cried out, 'I'm scar't that Diney Sue won't luff me because uff what I haf done!'

"There was another cry, except this time it was Diney Sue, sitting in a row behind Big Dietrich's family. She leaped out of her seat, made it past the folks around her, pushed past the deputy trying to hold her back, and rushed into Big Dietrich's arms like a young fawn being embraced by a big ol' grizzly.

"People was shouting and Judge Samuels was slamming his gavel down on the top his desk, and Big Dietrich was holding onto that little gal like she was life itself. Well, end result was that the judge let Big Dietrich go with a stern warning not to overdo defending himself from then on. He told the four fellers if they ever tried going after Dietrich again, he'd deal with them after Dietrich did, and as far as he was concerned, they was lower than a bullfrog's belly.

"Big Dietrich and Diney Sue was married a year or so later. He never did get rid of that scowl, and people still stepped aside when he rumbled into town. But, somehow things was different. We seen all along what Big Dietrich was like on the outside, but now we knew a bit more about what he was like on the inside, and he didn't seem all that mean."

The boy's mouth hung open as he stared up at the old man. The old man stretched out an arm and rumpled the boy's hair.

"So, boy, when you see old Homer here just a'layin' like a bump on a log, don't judge him too quickly. Appearances can be deceiving."

The boy spoke up then. "You mean, Homer's a fast old boy, Granpaw?"

The old man chuckled. "I didn't say that. Actually, you're right when you say Homer is lazy. But, listen now. Wait 'til ol' Homer watches a rabbit hop around in front of him before callin' him names. Ain't it better to judge someone by their actions 'stead of their looks? That goes for dogs and people alike, boy. People's too quick to judge others just 'cause of how they look. Give a feller a chance to show what he's made of before you go callin' him this or that."

The old man smiled as he saw understanding cross the boy's face. He reached over and poked him in the shoulder. "Now, how's about goin' in and gettin' your ol' Granpaw some lemonade to wet his whistle? Pour yourself a big glass too."

The boy scrambled up and ran into the cool of the house, the wooden screen door slamming shut behind him. The old man leaned back into the swing, his hand trailing down to scratch Homer behind the ears. The hound's tail began a slow thumping as the swing rocked back and forth, back and forth, back and forth.

# THE CHIEF'S GREATEST LOVE AFFAIR

*(The rock group Queen's song "We are the
Champions" was the inspiration for this story.)*

🏴 🏴 🏴

The Chief don't get around that much anymore. He mostly just sits in
a wooden chair in the shade of his trailer, gazing out over the cotton
fields and shaking his cane at any mockingbirds saucy enough to land on
his tomato plants or sunflowers.

Granddad got his nickname because of his years in the U.S. Navy, and
his rank when he retired – chief petty officer. That's the same as a sergeant
first class in the Army.

The Chief enlisted in the Navy when the U.S. entered World War I. He
was only 15 but was a big fella and lied about his age to the recruiter, so he
got in. He served aboard a four-stack destroyer that helped escort convoys
of troop ships across the North Atlantic to England. He got partial credit
for sinking a German U-boat when his destroyer depth-charged a sub to
the surface and his gun crew sunk it with a barrage of three-inch shells.

In 1921, during liberty on the coast of Norway, he got his first tattoo,
a big American flag on his left shoulder. He added other tattoos over the
years – "Consuela" in Madrid, "Francois" in Marseilles, "Chithra" in
Dublin and "Francesca" in Naples. There was other tattoos but the one he
was always most proud of was that American flag flying on his shoulder.

He got "Chang Li" tattooed when he was on an American gunboat
patrolling the Yangtze River in China. What with the various warlords

and bandits and international bickering, he saw his share of action aboard his boat and on landing parties.

He was there that Sunday morning in Pearl Harbor. First he grabbed a 40mm gun and when he run out of ammo, got an M-1 rifle and fired away at the dive bombers and torpedo planes swooping overhead.

The Chief was on a destroyer at the battles of Coral Sea and Midway and in the waters around Guadalcanal and the Solomon Islands. He was on the USS Johnston off the Philippine Islands when a handful of destroyers threw themselves between the aircraft carriers they was protecting and a bunch of Jap battleships and heavy cruisers. When shells the size of oil drums slammed into the Johnston and sent it under, he was among the handful of surviving crewmembers that spent hours in waters filled with sharks. There were a lot fewer sailors by the time they were rescued.

The Chief hardly got a breath after World War II before the Communist North Koreans attacked into South Korea. He was in his 50s then but he did his part, watching over gun crews on destroyers escorting American aircraft carriers as they launched attacks on advancing Communist armies. His destroyer was there pumping shells ashore when General Macarthur's troops did their end-around at Inchon.

They made The Chief retire in 1967. His final tour of duty was aboard the aircraft carrier USS Independence off the coast of South Vietnam. He always said if the Navy had let him stay in a bit longer, he coulda helped turn things around in Vietnam.

Not that he didn't get more involved anyway. Mom and Pop had talked him into moving in with us on our farm along the Loosahatchie River bottoms, One sumner day in '69, when protests against the Vietnam War was going strong, The Chief and a couple of his veteran buddies took me to the zoo in Memphis. I was just a little tyke then.

We spent a day at the zoo and was walking' toward the parking lot when we heard a commotion farther into the park. The Chief's nose started twitching' like a hound dog's on a scent of a raccoon. He and his buddies headed over to the crowd, dragging me along.

There was four or five scraggedy-looking fellas shouting about the U.S. being all mean and evil. Then they held up the American flag and lit a match to it, and The Chief began moving forward. I tried to pull him back and pleaded with him that he'd get hurt. He just looked down at me and growled, "Sonny, I'll burn in hell before I stand by and let them burn our country's flag."

He lit out into those protesters, and his buddies joined in the fracas. By the time the police arrived, those military veterans had those scraggly-looking fellas on the ground begging for mercy.

The Chief carried the flag, a bit burned at one corner, over to me and said, "Sonny, help me fold Old Glory." So, the two of us folded our nation's flag, using the trifold method him and me had both learned in the Boy Scouts. He brought it back to the farm with us, and raised that flag every day from then on from a pole in front of his trailer.

You could say The Chief went to sea again one more time, and he took the flag with him. It was the Fourth of July in 1983. He was 81 then but darned if he didn't enter the rowboat race at the local Independence Day festivities. Folks got a laugh out of his entering the race but when he showed up with that flag flying from the stern of his rowboat, the laughter eased off considerably. There was about a dozen fellas in that race – The Chief and a bunch of strapping young farm boys. Them farm boys was racing toward the finish line with The Chief far behind, huffing an' puffing. One of the contestants said something to the others and they all turned their boats around and headed back toward The Chief. They gathered their boats around his and pushed him toward the finish line so he crossed first. The Chief didn't say nothing, just sat there erect and strong. A little puff of wind caught up the flag and made it ripple some as it and The Chief finished first.

That was my granddad's last hurrah. He kept busy with his garden and puttering around the farm doing odd jobs and errands and chores. From time to time, we'd take him to the nursing home to visit with his veteran buddies, who continued to dwindle in numbers.

He kept slowing down, and had his first stroke in 1986. He came to live with me and my family then, since Mom and Pop was getting a bit old themselves to take care of him. The Chief mostly just sits around now dozing and dreaming and remembering. We feed him and bathe him and help him in and out of his trailer and his rocking chair.

One thing me and my wife and kids are careful about. On special occasions like Veterans Day and Memorial Day and Independence Day and Flag Day, we make sure The Chief hears us coming when we head back toward his trailer to see how he's doing.

After all, it wouldn't do for us to catch The Chief with a tear in his eye as he squints up at the flagpole and sees, flying proudly in the breeze, the Stars and Stripes, still and always the biggest love of his life.

⚑   ⚑   ⚑

# Miss Eugenia's Graduation Day Dragons

Only seven of us from the class of 1925 were left last year to honor Miss Eugenia. I expect that number will have been whittled down some when we meet again next week.

A factory that builds computer parts stands where Loosahatchie County Consolidated School District High School used to be. The magnolia tree the class of '26 planted still shades that little corner of grass and flowers at the edge of the factory's parking lot. The county keeps it mowed and weeded and watered.

Miss Eugenia was as much a fixture at Loosahatchie County School as the bicycle racks out front and the bell that clanged to announce the start of classes, recess, lunch and the end of the day. Like the bike racks, she was bent and worn, but she kept right on doing her job. Like the bell, she was a vital part of our day.

Miss Eugenia worked in the school cafeteria. She had helpers but for generations of children, she <u>was</u> the cafeteria. Miss Eugenia made biscuits so light they could have floated across the lunchroom. Her pork chops and fried chicken were so tasty, the older kids said pigs and chickens stood in line just for the honor of stepping into her big industrial sized skillets. She cooked vegetables in a way the younger children actually went back for seconds. And her desserts; oh, my. My brother said angels hung around the kitchen door hoping for a taste of her chocolate cakes, peach cobblers and pecan pies.

She was the ruler of the cafeteria but Miss Eugenia was a benevolent ruler. She did more than cook. She was smiles, hugs and laughter. She always had time to walk among the tables, teasing here, joking there. She made lunch a form of entertainment.

Her love for us and our for her extended beyond the lunchroom. She'd often be at the front entrance when we came to school to help us shake off rainy jackets or shed muddy galoshes. A girl crying at recess would find her sadness whisked away by a hug from Miss Eugenia, who always seemed to materialize from nowhere at just the right moment. In the morning we could hear her laughter dancing down the halls from the kitchen, and in the afternoon her singing wafted through open windows. Students went to her with problems and she had a way to lift any worry.

That spring of 1925, she wound up having an impact on the entire county when the school board announced she had been asked to give the main speech at our graduation ceremonies. It was the topic of conversation throughout Loosahatchie County. In feedlots, offices, sharecropper shacks and stately mansions, on sidewalks and backroads, folks buzzed until the entire county sounded like a giant beehive.

There were the usual letters to school board members and the county newspaper, ugly anonymous letters written by brave individuals who used terms like "nigger" and "nigger lover." Most people, though -- some perhaps with a little misgiving -- accepted the idea that a black person would be the first graduation speaker in the history of our school district. We students were delighted. Miss Eugenia was our confidante and trusted advisor. She was our friend.

We'd seen signs of her problems in the weeks before graduation night. She had walked more slowly and breathed with a bit of a wheeze. That evening in the school gymnasium, we sat in our rows of folding metal chairs and worried up at an empty seat on the stage behind the podium. The principal waited until everyone was seated and then announced that Miss Eugenia had been taken sick and one of the county commissioners would be giving the main address.

He had barely begun speaking when the outside doors of the gymnasium banged open and there stood two of Miss Eugenia's grandsons. Between them was Miss Eugenia, wheezing and trembling. You could hear the ceiling fans' rhythmic clicking as her escorts helped her shuffle down the middle of the gym floor, past the capped and gowned teens who would be receiving our diplomas that evening, and, up in the bleachers, our families and friends.

Commissioner Sanders and Principal Myers helped ease Miss Eugenia up the few steps to the stage and to the podium. Reverend Kelley hauled up a couple more chairs and the grandsons sat down with the others on the stage.

Miss Eugenia smiled out over this latest in dozens of classes she had seen graduate, then started to speak in a voice that, though it wavered, was remarkably loud and clear.

"Chilluns," she began – She always called us that, from the tiniest first grader to the most hulking 12th grade football player. -- "chilluns, they aksed me to be heah tonight an' I promised I would, so here I be. I been thinkin' long an' hard on what to say to y'all. I don' know nuthin' 'bout high-falutin' goals an' ambitions an' other fancy things a real speaker would talk to you 'bout this evenin'. But I do have this."

She paused to reach into a pocket on her dress and pull out a piece of paper.

"Some years on back, I chanced to read me a book written 'bout those days that had knights and dragons an' such. An' this one line jumped out to me. It be from a poem 'bout a knight struck down in a ferocious battle."

She held the piece of paper close to her face since she evidently didn't have her reading glasses with her, and read, "I will lay me down to bleed awhile, and then arise and fight again."

She put the piece of paper back in her pocket and looked down at us. I felt she was looking right at me. Over the years, others have told me they felt she was staring straight at them.

"Chilluns, this life ain't easy. It's full o' pain an' sufferin'. They gonna be times you gonna get knocked down hard. Ain't no mo' dragons on this earth but there be other ways you be made to suffer. Could be a storm wipe out your crop o' cotton. Could be a water moccasin bite dead your favorite huntin' dog. Could be a fire burn your home to the ground. Could be a little gal or a little fella your pride and joy die from the fever.

"When that happens, you go on ahead an' lay you down an' bleed awhile. You go ahead an' feel the miserables an' suffer hard an' have a good cry. That's alright. Don't let no one tell you how long you should lie there or how you should feel. That be up to you.

"But then," – At this point, she suddenly slammed her fist onto the podium with such a resounding crash, I don't think there wasn't a person in that gymnasium who didn't lift off their seat at least two inches. – "You 'arise an' fight again.' There be a time for mournin' an' a time for a'getting' back on yo' feet. Sure, life have its pains an' hurts, but life be good. You fight the dragons when you got to, an' take the licks ever'one takes, but keep in mind the love an' laughter an' friendship an' churchgoin' an' get-togethers at Christmas an' Thanksgivin' an' clean wash flappin' in the breeze an' the scent of rich dirt an' th' taste of nickel candy an' fried chicken an' honest work an' gran'parents an' good neighbors an' …"

She began wheezing again. It was a moment before she could continue.

"Tha's all ah have t' say. Jus' 'member, all through y'all's life, 'I will lay me down to bleed awhile, and then arise and fight again.'"

She motioned to her grandsons and they fairly leaped from their seats to help her sit down. Applause should follow a speech but once again all you could hear was the ticking of the ceiling fans. Somehow, though, that silence seemed more deafening than a standing ovation.

Miss Eugenia recovered from her illness and continued working her wonders in the school cafeteria. As for the class of 1925, we never forgot her words to us that muggy May evening in the Loosahatchie County High School gymnasium. Through layoffs and labor pains, deaths and divorce, separations and sickness, we remembered that it was all right to lay down and bleed awhile and cry too, but then there was a time to get back up and look out at the birds that continued to sing and the flowers that continued to bloom, and keep going. The time I needed the comfort of her words the most, that afternoon by the family pond when I watched them recover my son from the water and a part of my heart ripped away, Miss Eugenia's words settled softly on my bowed shoulders. At that moment, even though I would grieve for a long time after, the healing process had already begun.

As a gift to the school, the class of '25 had a cement bench placed in a corner of the front lawn. On one pedestal leg was carved a picture of a knight fighting a dragon. The other pedestal leg bears an image of Miss Eugenia hugging a child. The bench seat bears the inscription, "I will lay me down to bleed awhile, and then arise and fight again."

That wasn't all, though. It took a lot of fast wrangling and wading through red tape, but when Miss Eugenia passed away in 1937, we got special permission to bury her alongside that bench of hers. That made the memorial complete, there in front of the school where she had tended so long and so well to our stomachs, our hearts and our souls.

Funny thing, though. Among the hundreds of names on the petition we got up asking for the special burial site were several signatures remarkably similar to the handwriting on those ugly anonymous letters written a dozen years before.

# THE POLICEMAN WHO CRIED

The rest of us on the force should have realized Johnson was cracking up. We might have been able to prevent what happened.

It was the spring of '54. I was fresh home from Korea and with my MP background got a job with the Winterdale Police Department. They teamed me up with a 36-year veteran of the force, Lieutenant Kendall Johnson. Johnson was a widower with two grown children and five grandchildren. He loved those grandkids. Any off-duty day, the youngsters were at Gramps' house or he was at their homes. In the summer he took them fishing and camping and hiking. In the winter, they made brownies in his kitchen, or played board games in the living room, or built birdhouses and toys out in his workshop.

We have our share of crime in Winterdale. Not as bad as in the city, of course, but it's there. In my first year patrolling with Johnson, we handled a fair number of burglaries, a bounced check or two, several assaults, a few stills, fights at the honky tonks on the edge of town, and some domestic disputes.

Through it all, Johnson was the crackerjack professional; doing it by the book, smooth, efficient. There was one type of call, though, that seemed to rattle him some; domestic disputes involving kids. When we had a situation in which a child had witnessed his parents fighting or, worse still, got in the middle of it and wound up with a black eye or split lip, Johnson seemed to take it personal. More than once, I had to tell him to ease up when he was cuffing a stepfather or boyfriend, or taking him out to the unit.

One time I was already out of the house with the mother and her son.

The boy had a broken arm and a number of bruises. It was several minutes before Johnson came down from the second story and out on the porch with the boyfriend. That guy's face was puffed up, one eye was black and his nose was bleeding. Johnson said he fell down the stairs. He looked hard at the boyfriend when he said that, and the man sort of shook and didn't say anything.

One night we were out at the far end of town watching for speeders when the call came in for a unit to respond to an alleged child beating at the other end of town. A couple of the other boys answered that one. For the next half hour we listened to the two-way tell the story; the initial report of screaming coming from the house, the arrival on scene of two units, the call for an ambulance, and the transporting of both parents to jail on charges of assaulting their own three-year-old.

Johnson had me driving that night. I was listening to the radio and clocking passing motorists when I heard a sob. I glanced over. The flickering red light of a nearby motel sign was shining on tears streaming down Johnson's face. He noticed me staring before I quick turned back to the road ahead. He reached for his handkerchief.

He cursed quietly as he wiped his face, sighed deeply, and looked over at me.

"It's not right, Wagner," he said. "Things like that. They shouldn't happen. To adults, maybe. That's life. But not kids, not children."

His voice choked and he looked down the dark road.

"Someday," he whispered, "someday …"

Someday was two weeks later. Johnson and I answered a call to a home in a quiet little, white collar neighborhood just off the main drag. The first grade teacher at the grade school had reported seven-year-old Lizzy Bateman hadn't been at school that day after coming to class the day before with two black eyes. Her father had a reputation for having a temper, and the teacher had a hunch.

As we walked up the front steps, a window curtain moved aside just for a moment. When we knocked, Mr. Bateman answered. He was breathing heavily.

"What the hell do you want?" he snarled.

From out of a hall door behind him, his daughter staggered into view. She was covered with blood.

Johnson put his shoulder to Bateman, sending him crashing to the floor, and rushed to the little girl. She collapsed into his arms. As he carried her out the door, he shouted at me, "Cuff him and wait here! I'll call for backup!"

The old county hospital was four miles from the Bateman home. The police dispatcher recorded Johnson's 10-8 at 9:11 and his 10-7 at the hospital at 9:15. The doctors later testified they counted and treated 129 cigarette burns on Lizzy's torso, arms and legs.

Johnson arrived at the station just as we were finishing booking Bateman and taking him to his cell. There were nine of us at the station at that moment but it took us several minutes to get Johnson off Bateman. Bateman hired a hotshot lawyer and got off with court costs and probation. Johnson got a hearing and was removed from the force.

I stopped by to see him a few times in the following weeks but he acted like he didn't want company. I talked with his son and daughter and they said something seemed to have gone out of him; that he wasn't seeing the grandkids that much anymore.

A month passed. Word got out Harold Bateman was back at it with his little girl but he was too smart to get caught this time. And, he had his wife too cowed to do anything. She always wore sunglasses out in public, even in rainy weather. Then one day a fieldhand found Bateman out on his farm, lying against a corncrib, a bullet hole between the eyes.

Chief Furr went out to talk to former lieutenant Kendall Johnson. The chief was in Johnson's house for close to four hours. A couple weeks later, the case was closed. They never did find out who killed Bateman.

Bateman's death seemed to bring Johnson out of his self-imposed solitude. He went back to seeing his grandchildren on a regular basis. The grandkids were glad to have their old granddad back.

Twelve years passed. Johnson's daughter and daughter-in-law stopped by one Saturday morning in 1966 to do some housecleaning for the retired patrolman. They found him lying out in his workshop next to an almost-finished dollhouse. The coroner said it had been a massive heart attack, and death had been instantaneous. He was buried in the Winterdale City

Cemetery. With their parents help, his grandkids finished building the dollhouse. They donated it to an orphanage.

I retired from the police department five years ago. I go out to the city cemetery every Sunday afternoon to be sure Johnson's plot is kept up. A lot of the time, Elizabeth Bateman Coolidge is out there too, putting fresh flowers on the grave or trimming the grass around the headstone. Even in the hottest weather, Mrs. Coolidge wears long sleeves. I guess she's still self-conscious about some of those 129 scars showing on her arms.

We talk some, and listen to the wind sighing through the trees and the headstones there on the hill, and silently reread the inscription on the headstone: "Kendall Johnson, 1897-1966, Beloved Father and Grandfather, Police Officer, Protector of Children"

I often think of what I did. I did it not only to protect Mrs. Bateman and her little girl, but also to protect Kendall Johnson. He was my friend and my partner. I didn't want Harold Bateman's death to be on Kendall's conscience, so I had to get to Bateman before he did.

# ABOUT THE AUTHOR

Chuck Warzyn has been a writer all of his professional career - as a ship's journalist and public affairs officer in the United States Navy, publications coordinator for a multi-state health care system, county 4-H program coordinator, and state case manager for foster parents. He has written numerous articles that have appeared in newspapers and magazines around the U.S. Other than a Navy cruise book, this is the first time his work has appeared in book form.

In addition to drawing on his professional experiences, Mr. Warzyn has also obtained ideas for his writing from the world of music, and from volunteer activities, including being a foster parent for more than 60 children and fostering more than 100 dogs for humane societies over the years, assisting at animal shelters, and participating in nursing home pet therapy.

Mr. Warzyn received his bachelor's degree in English from the University of Missouri in 1973. He attended the Defense Information School at Fort Benjamin Harrison in Indianapolis, where he completed programs in print, photo and broadcast journalism.

He was born in Illinois, grew up in Missouri, and has lived in Indiana, California and Tennessee. He currently resides in Georgia.

Mr. Warzyn is dedicating "Stories for the Seasons" to individuals and groups throughout the United States and around the world who are working to reduce the suffering of animals. He is donating 10 percent of his profits from this book to his local humane society, 10 percent will go to the American Society for the Prevention of Cruelty to Animals, and 10 percent will be donated to the World Society for the Protection of Animals.

Mr. Warzyn's favorite Bible verse is Matthew 25:40 -- "Inasmuch as ye have done it unto one of the least of these my brethren, ye have done it unto me."

LaVergne, TN USA
20 January 2011
213293LV00004B/4/P